CHEERLEADERS

#6

SPLITTING

JENNIFER SARASIN

D0711982

SCHOLASTIC INC.
New York Toronto London Auckland Sydney Tokyo

ISBN 0-590-33407-7

Published by Scholastic Inc.

12 11 10 9 8 7 6 5 4 3 2 1   6   5 6 7 8 9/8 0/9

Printed in the U.S.A.   01

CHEERLEADERS

SPLITTING

CHEERLEADERS

CHAPTER 1

Pres was really out of it. It was a conscious effort, not to listen to his father, but he could do it. He could sit and actually look at him, actually seem as though his gaze were riveted on his father's face, when in reality his mind was on a game or a sexy girl or adjusting the valves on his Porsche. There wasn't much to it, really. Just send your mind out of the dining room, past the maid standing in the doorway with crystal bowls full of chocolate-mint ice cream, and let it go careening into space.

"And we've made a superlative profit, just on this month's statement alone." Preston Tilford II leaned back contentedly in his chair and watched as the dessert dish was placed before him.

"Wonderful, dear." Pres's mother wasn't looking adoringly at her husband's steel-gray eyes or gray hair, though. She was looking at her son, her black-sheep cheerleader son. If only he would

1

respond a little — not even with enthusiasm, but just with mild interest.

Pres's eyes were closed now. He took a mouthful of ice cream and concentrated on separating out the chocolate chips. It was like dividing the Oreos when he was a kid, saving the side with the filling for last. He sure wasn't a kid anymore. He was nearly eighteen, but he felt older, as if he'd been through a lot — except when he was driving the Porsche, or hanging out with Kerry, or cheering with the team. He imagined them standing in a circle around the circumference of his dessert bowl — Mary Ellen the lovely, Nancy the sexy, Angie the dependable, Olivia the silent, and good old slaphappy Walt.

"So, Pres," his father continued. "I'll tell you, even though you haven't asked. Martin's promised that you can start with Investment Services in three weeks. He's going to give you all the training you need. If you won't come to work for me at Tarenton Fabricators, at least we can drill some financial expertise into you. Of course, it will mean giving up all extracurricular activities, including that . . . that team you're on."

Pres's mind slowly returned to the room, then jerked to attention. "What are you talking about?"

"It's about time you took some real responsibility." His father nodded with that little half smile of his that never quite reached his eyes. "And gave up those stupid games you play after school." He hated the notion of his son as a cheerleader so much that he couldn't even bring himself to say the word aloud. "This job will prepare you for the business courses you'll take in college."

Pres put his spoon down on the cherry wood table, his handsome face a frozen mask. For a second, he just sat there, trying not to let his anger show, trying not to let a single emotion out. "It's a joke, right? A funny joke?"

"No joke, Pres. Martin's made you a firm offer."

"Well, why didn't Martin tell me? Isn't that the way jobs are usually handled? When you don't have pull, I mean. When you're not trying to find your idiot son some paper-pushing, boring, stupid way to occupy his time." He gathered steam like a locomotive.

His mother let out a long sigh, then covered her face with her hands.

"I don't like your tone," Mr. Tilford said with deadly calm.

"I don't like the way you treat me, Dad." Pres stood up, his six-foot frame seeming taller in the candlelight. The maid, standing in the doorway holding the silver coffee service, flew back into the kitchen. "I don't have to take this, not anymore. I'm old enough — nearly eighteen. I'm getting out, man. I mean *out*!"

He pushed his knees back against the upholstered chair, feeling power and strength surging through him. The chair hit the floor, but he didn't bother to right it. He kept walking, though he wanted to run. Run and crawl under the covers like a kid, but he couldn't do that anymore. He stalked to the hallway, grabbed his keys from the marble-topped table, and was out the

3

door before his parents could follow. He didn't know where he was going at this hour of night. Just driving, probably. He hardly heard his mother yelling, "Stop him, Preston! Oh, for heaven's sake! Baby, come back!"

No more baby. Not for him.

The crowd was great today. The stands were packed, despite the cold, and the mood was really high. After all, the Tarenton Wolves didn't play the Deep River Killers every day, so it was an event. Now, at halftime, the score was tied, right after Johnny Elliott had tackled the Deep River quarterback, forcing him to fumble the ball, which Bump Daniels recovered and carried over the goal line.

"Boy, did you see that?" Mary Ellen Kirkwood's brilliant cheerleader smile was for real as she raced, arm in arm with Pres, to take her place for the first cheer. Her honey-blonde hair blew attractively across her face, and she didn't bother to brush it away. As involved as Mary Ellen was, she never forgot how she looked. It was one of the most important things in life to her.

"Bump is *on*, man! I mean, the guy's a miracle worker!" Walt Manners didn't usually get this excited about football, but there was something different about him today. He raised Angie Poletti in an impromptu shoulder-sit and she giggled happily.

"Put her down, Walt." Nancy Goldstein tugged at his arm. "Time to get to work."

"Yeah." Olivia Evans, the smallest member

4

of the cheerleading team, took her place, arching into an effortless backbend in front of the group. "I'm freezing. Let's get this over with."

The crowd's excitement hadn't abated one bit as the Tarenton squad assembled for their opening cheer, a splashy number that Angie and Nancy had choreographed one rainy day. The girls' scarlet skirts swayed in the light wind, revealing their white pleats. Each of the four of thcm revelled in the outfit, the white V-neck sweater with its scarlet bands and the proud "T" on the front, completing the perfect look that made them one.

The boys hoisted Olivia by all four limbs and spun her as Mary Ellen did a triple cartwheel that ended in a split. Olivia gracefully managed to slip to the ground in time to perform a meticulous series of back flips with the other three girls, while the boys stag-leaped around them.

"We're gonna win it, gonna beat 'em, gonna
    shine,
We're the team that's putting all the other
    guys in line.
We can go . . . (stamp, stamp) hot!
We can run . . . (clap, clap) wild!
We can WIN! We can WIN!"

The spectacular close called for super-human energy on everyone's part. Pres was to sweep Nancy up through a pirouette into a flying mount to his shoulders, Angie and Mary Ellen were to form a handstand arch in front of Walt, and Olivia was to do two straddle jumps and end up

5

in a split on the ground, her hands raised in the air in triumph.

But even as they were moving, Mary Ellen sensed something odd. What was it? She prided herself on always getting the big picture on a scene. Even when she was concerned with herself, with her looks, with what other people thought about her, she could still make sense of things.

She knew something was wrong, and looked to Nancy for confirmation even as she bobbed over into a handstand. Then she heard Nancy gasp and saw her falling, away from Pres. She landed with a hard clunk on the gravel, and there was an almost indiscernible streak of blood along her left thigh. Although Mary Ellen saw pain behind the other girl's eyes, Nancy recovered beautifully. Her tawny complexion was slightly paler, but she was smiling, just the way Ardith Engborg, their coach, always insisted upon.

"What the. . . ?" Walt muttered in annoyance. He didn't like Pres all of the time, mostly because Pres took the easy way out. Walt, who came on like the class clown, was enormously serious underneath. He'd die rather than shirk responsibility. Or drop a girl in full sight of the entire school.

Unfortunately, the team wasn't alone in picking up on the slip. The front bleachers in the stands were practically right over their heads. Susan Yardley and her boyfriend Jimmy stood up in horror as they saw Nancy take the fall, and Vanessa Barlow and her two Deep River boyfriends laughed out loud. Vanessa was the daughter of the superintendent of schools, which made her think that the world of Tarenton High revolved around her needs and wishes. What she seemed to wish, mostly, was for every girl on the cheerleading team to be dropped through a hole in the earth, so that she could take all their glory. But one down would do.

Pres just stood there, his face blank.

"Keep going, for heaven's sake!" Angie hissed at him.

"What's wrong, Pres? C'mon, we just started." Olivia, always thought of as the most retiring one of the team, could speak up when she had to. Her mother had learned this recently, much to her dismay. Because Olivia had suffered from a heart condition as a child, she'd been smothered with care in the name of love until she'd joined this team. Then, and only then, had she found the will and way to strike out on her own.

Olivia bodily swung Pres around into the second cheer, leading the others. Her tiny 90-pound frame seemed to grow larger as she hauled his large one into action.

"Harass them, harass them,
Make them relinquish the ball!"

Mary Ellen started the "vocabulary cheer," as they called it back in the locker room, and the others joined in loudly. Angie, always the one to try to smooth over a difficult spot, added a pike to her part of the routine, following it with a graceful back walkover. Anything to take the crowd's focus off Pres, Angie thought.

Angie was a peacemaker at heart, the joy of

her big sprawling family. Her mother, Rose, had carried on with her life when her husband died, and worked her way up to owning her own beauty parlor while raising three kids at the same time. Her mother could hoist the weight of the world on her shoulders, but Angie could take the same weight and make it look effortless, smiling, always helpful, extremely popular.

The five of them moved around Pres, pushing him into position, jostling him into doing his part of the routine. But as halftime progressed, it became obvious to the crowd that they were working against an immovable force.

"Poor Pres," Vanessa Barlow said, loud enough for her entire section to hear. "He must have been struck by lightning. He's *sooo* electrifying!" Her peal of nasty laughter coated the air like a thick, cloying syrup.

"Hey, if this is what Tarenton has to offer, they better get the stiffs off the field," one of her Deep River bozos guffawed. "Gimme a team of girl cheerleaders any day — right, Van?" He nudged her in the ribs so hard she nearly fell off her seat.

"I don't know. These girls never impressed me as anything much," she shrugged.

Nancy glared up at Vanessa even as she sprang into a spread-eagle jump, reaching her arms to the heavens and smiling, always smiling. "Don't let her get to you," she hissed through her teeth at Pres. "For heaven's sake, shape up, will you?"

"Leave me alone," Pres demanded. He took her wrist and swung her around so hard, he left burns on her smooth skin.

8

The last routine was over. The team took a perfunctory bow in their toughest position — a pyramid that fell over into multiple cartwheels — and ran to the sidelines, as much to hide their chagrin as to make way for the football players.

"I don't get you at all, man," Walt said angrily to Pres, as they waited for the first play before they started working the crowd. It was their job to keep the enthusiasm high throughout the game, regardless of what was going on.

"What's to get? I'm just a little bored today." Pres's crooked smile darkened his handsome face.

"We've all got our problems," Olivia reminded him. "But they're not supposed to show when we're performing. How many times has Ardith been over that with us?" After years of struggling back from illness, Olivia was the toughest of them all.

"Don't hound him." Mary Ellen wasn't watching Tarenton's particularly bad skirmish; she was worried about Pres. If there was anything she wanted in life, besides escape from this hick town and her poverty, it was a boy like Pres. Maybe Pres himself, if he'd start asking her out again. It wasn't that she was bored with Donny Parrish, captain of the Tarenton basketball team, but Pres was something different. Donny was a lapdog at her feet; Pres was the dangerous cougar, standing at the top of the mountain, daring her to chase him down.

Angie let out a sigh of frustration and gave the high sign to Kimberley, the leader of the twelve-member Pompon Squad, to start encouraging the crowd. "Let's discuss this later," Mary Ellen said to Pres.

"I don't want to. As a matter of fact," Pres said with grim determination, "I don't want to do anything right now. How about that?" And with no warning at all, he walked off the field. Just kept walking, slowly and steadily, out around the bleachers and back to the parking lot. No one could stop him. No one would dare.

The other five halted only a moment before renewing their efforts to get the audience excited. It was no use, though. Tarenton, for some reason, was losing miserably to Deep River. Nancy couldn't help but think that *they* had done it, that the cheerleaders had let the ball players down and ruined the whole game. Was it possible? Well, Ardith would certainly say it was.

So they tried harder — even when it started to rain, even when the Wolves let Deep River make three field goals in a row, and Bump Daniels completely missed two easy lateral passes. What else could they do but band together, trying to pretend they were still a squad.

The Wolves lost the game, 21 to 18, and the feeling in the locker room afterward was intense. A cold wind swept through them, even inside the steamy hall where they congregated like lost sheep to receive Mrs. Engborg's admonishment.

"Who'd like to explain?" The small ball of fury who was their coach and their inner conscience stood before them, looking about twice her normal height. She was a wiry blonde in her forties, the toughest taskmaster any of them had ever worked for.

10

There was silence. People stared at the floor or at the door. Walt chewed his gum noisily and Mary Ellen curled the tendrils that crept around her lovely, high cheekbones.

"I saw Pres burn rubber out of the parking lot right after halftime." Ardith bit the words off. "I saw him drop Nancy, too. You know, I don't have a clue as to what you think you're here for, but Varsity means something to me. And if one of you goes off the deep end, that's no excuse. Everyone else is supposed to pick him up and carry on. Ever think of that? No, none of you escape blame for today. Don't look away, Nancy — it's your fault as much as anyone's. And yours, Angie. What about you, Olivia? You're the one with the discipline, aren't you? And why didn't you get Pres back, Walt? Why didn't you cover for him, Mary Ellen? I want answers here." Her hazel eyes took on each of them individually, two lazer beams that pierced their very souls.

"We fell down on the job, I guess," Nancy muttered. She had a terrible fear that, having come so far, she was about to be ditched for this one offense. It wasn't easy, wanting to be part of this group the way she did. Nancy still sometimes felt like an outsider, one of the few Jewish girls in the school, and she needed to be here.

"I'm disgusted with all of you. I'll speak with Pres Monday, but I expect one or all of you to get hold of him this weekend. This is supposed to be teamwork, in case you've forgotten." Ardith marched off down the corridor, shaking her head.

"Who wants to drive over to Pres's house?" Walt asked. "We can all pile into my Jeep."

11

"No, that's like ganging up on him," Angie argued.

"I'm too tired for a fight now, anyway," Olivia declared, swinging her gym bag over her shoulder.

"Except for a good knock-down drag-out with your mom," Walt countered.

Olivia didn't know how to take that at first, not until she saw the sly smile spreading over his face. Walt liked the fact that she stood up to her mother. She barely returned his smile, but their eyes met and held, a new admiration growing between them.

"I've got to get home," Nancy said. "Anybody need a ride?" She was secretly as thrilled that she was now able to borrow her mother's car and drive alone, as she had been to get on the Varsity Squad. This year's birthday present — private driving lessons — had been her most cherished gift in years.

Mary Ellen hesitated just a minute before accepting the ride. It was the worst embarrassment of her life to have to bum rides from everyone, but Donny had the flu, so she was stuck. The only other alternative was waiting around until her dad finished his bus route and picked her up. That could mean hours of hanging out, letting people know she was so poor she could only afford public transportation when her father was driving it. If she waited too long, Patrick Henley would be sure to appear, eager and willing to escort her home in his garbage truck. Patrick, who loved her, who would probably lay down his life for her. She was terribly attracted to him, and was constantly fighting her feelings for him. How

12

could she fall in love with a guy who was proud of his father's garbage business, and even prouder of the fact that he'd earned enough money to buy his own truck? The trash man — how could he be the heartthrob she was waiting for?

"Sure, I'd love it," she said to Nancy, her brilliant blue eyes grateful. "Why don't we all talk tomorrow? Maybe one of us can go see Pres and hash this out."

As they straggled to the parking lot together, they each had their separate moments of selfish concern. It seemed so unfair, really, to get blamed for something someone else had done. They'd always had trouble being a team, banding together — Ardith was right about that. But this was Pres's craziness, not theirs.

"See you, guys," Walt waved as he climbed into his Jeep.

" 'Bye, see you Monday," Angie called as her older brother, Al, honked his horn and she ran, smiling again, toward his car.

Olivia, bundled up to the hilt, walked to the bike rack where she removed the heavy lock from her Atala five-speed. Until there was snow on the ground, she rode that thing all over Tarenton, just to show everyone she could. She had just stuck her gym bag in her basket and thrust her leg over the seat when she heard the sound of an engine right beside her.

"That bike'll fit right along the back of the Jeep," Walt said. "No hassle."

She squinted up at him. "No thanks."

"The ground is wet. You'll slip."

"I never have before," she assured him.

Walt took a deep breath. Why was he trying so hard? And with Olivia, of all people. "C'mon, will ya? Stop tap-dancing and let me give you a ride. I'll feel like I've done something right today, at least."

Her piercing dark eyes took him in, appraising him. Then she shrugged. "If you want." She watched him jump down from the driver's seat and slide the back door open. Then, without waiting for him to come around to her, she climbed in on the passenger side and let him stow her bike. She felt like a long ride, pedaling slowly through the light rain, but she also felt like talking to someone. It was a weird feeling, and she wondered why she'd given in to it. Olivia rarely let her feelings get the better of her.

Nancy watched Walt and Olivia start out of the parking lot, and she shook her head curiously. She looked over at Mary Ellen, but she apparently hadn't noticed anything, so Nancy didn't comment. She got behind the steering wheel and leaned over to unlock the other door for her passenger. But they'd waited too long. Vanessa Barlow was just climbing into the bucket seat of her latest guy's Camaro.

"Well, you all certainly made a spectacle of yourselves today," she smirked as the big lug beside her started the engine. "If I were a member of the squad, I'd have died of shame."

"Don't hold your breath, Vanessa," Nancy offered. "Since your best doesn't approximate our worst, I don't think there's any danger of your replacing one of us."

Vanessa shook her thick, dark hair over one

14

shoulder with a careless laugh. She swept her cashmere scarf gracefully around her neck, wrapping herself in yards of heather as she snuggled deeper into her warm antique raccoon coat. "You don't think I'm still pining to be on your little old team, do you? Mary Ellen, I can't imagine changing places with you. I mean, I wouldn't want to ride in the cab of someone's smelly garbage truck or live in a little turquoise house." With that, she gave her driver the high sign and they took off doing forty, screaming with laughter.

Mary Ellen sat straighter in her seat, pretending she hadn't heard. If only Vanessa's snipes could roll off her instead of sticking through her like tiny poison darts.

"She's so ridiculous, she's not even funny," Nancy snorted, pressing down on the accelerator. The car grumbled, refusing to turn over. "It's not even worth thinking up junk to throw back at her, you know?" She looked at her passenger out of the corner of her eye, knowing how much it hurt.

"Let's go, okay?" Mary Ellen said in a wan voice. "I'm really beat."

Nancy turned the key again, and this time, her efforts were rewarded. She couldn't help thinking as they drove off, though, that Mary Ellen's reaction was part of what was keeping the team apart. When you let things get to you, you could crumble to pieces like a kid's sandcastle. And then you were finished. She resolved to see Pres this weekend, and to turn him around.

CHAPTER

2

The dark-red Porsche careened up Fable Point, taking its own vengeance on the rutted road. Around the last point of the lake, and then, home. Pres laughed at that one. Home? It was ludicrous to even think of *that* place as a safe haven.

He didn't want to put the car in the drive — his father's drive — so he left it by the side of the road. He wouldn't be long, anyway. This was a perfect time to make a clean getaway, since his mother would be at the hairdresser's and his father always did some United Fund Drive charity thing on Saturday afternoons. No one around but the maid.

Even so, he used the back entrance. No need to call attention to himself. He took the back stairs up to his room and, without even thinking, grabbed his duffle bag out of the closet and started packing. As he shoved a pair of sneakers into the deep pocket of the bag, he felt like a man, a guy who could do as he pleased. He even had a place to stay; he'd been planning and thinking about it for weeks. So it was no big sweat — he'd just move out. Plenty of kids did it. Uncle James didn't know he was coming, but he was an okay guy who let things happen.

He threw clothes into the bag at random, trying not to let his mind work.

The other kids on the squad were furious with him, that went without saying. He knew he'd let them down, Nancy worst of all. He liked her, thought she was sexy as hell, even though he'd never asked her out. Maybe he should — maybe that would patch things up. But she didn't have a thing about him the way Mary Ellen did. Probably, of all of them, Mary Ellen would forgive him the quickest. He was kind of fascinated by her — she certainly was beautiful — but she was always trying for a goal she might never reach. Pres knew he was one of those goals, and he wasn't flattered by the idea. Mary Ellen didn't really pay attention to the present because she was so wrapped up in the future, she just couldn't wait to graduate and hightail it to New York and be a model. Well, she'd probably succeed, even if she had to scratch her way up by her long, polished fingernails.

If only Kerry had been at the game. She was visiting relatives this weekend, and had begged off, but at least he'd see her Monday at school. Kerry Elliot was a cool breeze in a dry desert for him: a soft girl, made of different textures and qualities. Only a sophomore, but wiser than

17

most seniors. He'd never known anyone like her before. Of course, his parents weren't wild about her, that also went without saying. You had to have a big bank account to please Preston Tilford II.

He zipped the case and tossed it casually over his shoulder, looking around the room once. There was his stereo and computer equipment. No, better to travel light. Anyhow, he didn't want the old man to say he'd ripped him off. It would be just like him to call the cops on his own son.

He was out the door, skimming down the staircase, out through the kitchen door, past the staircase, out through the kitchen door, past the have to cook for himself! What a laugh. Maybe he could get the team to come over and help. Nancy for meat loaf on Mondays, Olivia for chicken on Tuesdays, and so forth. Then he threw back his head and laughed. They probably didn't know how to cook any better than he did. Only Angie and Mary Ellen, whose parents had to dig for every dime, would know anything about the inside of a kitchen.

No regrets, he thought suddenly as he ran out the door and started up the Porsche again. It would be great, he decided, as he screeched off back around the lake. At least, he hoped it would be.

The Jeep lumbered down the road slowly like an old bear. It could go faster, but Walt didn't want it to. He wanted to savor this moment, this nice, quiet time to mellow out after the game.

"Hello, are you still there?" he asked.

18

Olivia gave him a look. "Can't you tell?"

"Sure. I can hear the click of the little wheels in your head a mile away."

She laughed, and it was a surprisingly cheery, almost childlike laugh. "Jeeps do it to me. I can't seem to stop thinking that we're about to hit a land mine or something."

"Only the ones the badgers laid. Don't worry, I'm a great driver." This was nice, Walt thought to himself. Cheerleading tired him out, even though he'd never let on. After all, he was The Amazing Rubber Man, the guy who bounced back. He was the happy-go-lucky gymnast who laughed at life and at himself. Why did he think it was nice with Olivia beside him? he wondered, sneaking a glance at her upright, stoic little profile.

He'd never noticed her much. She was great in performance, but sort of a drag at practice. Just like Ardith, always ready to work, always trying for the next hardest level. Tell her to do three scissor kicks, and she'd do six. Tell her to work on her aerial somersaults, and she'd keep going through dinner. A real hog for work. But Walt had been looking at her differently lately. Maybe somebody who worked so hard could play pretty hard, too. Maybe she could listen hard and pay attention to a guy who just didn't seem to draw girls like Pres did.

Olivia wasn't like the others on the squad, he decided. She wasn't concerned with her looks and what other people thought about her. She was just her own person.

"You live pretty deep in there, right?" Olivia

19

asked suddenly, pointing at the thick woods that skirted the lake. The trees were bare now, but you could still hardly see through the branches.

"Right. My folks built themselves this log fortress about ten years ago. Keeps out the elephants, at least."

"A good thing, too," Olivia nodded, playing along. "They do their morning TV show from there, don't they? Their interviews are pretty interesting. I've heard them sometimes, when I'm getting ready for school," she explained.

"Yeah, that's the only time I hear them. I think I've gotten so that I only understand what they're saying when they're talking into a mike. 'Oh, Walt, your mother would like you to empty the dishwasher,' he mimed a microphone in his left hand. 'Would you care to say a few words to the studio audience about that?' "

Olivia actually giggled. He'd never heard her giggle. "What's it like having parents who are celebrities?"

"They're not . . . I mean, just because people know their faces doesn't mean they're the Jackson Two or anything." He shrugged and put the Jeep in first as they struggle up a hill. "One thing, though. They're a team. They work together, eat together, live together. Sometimes I watch them, you know, and I feel kind of —" He stopped midsentence, and she jumped in.

"Superfluous? I feel like that around my mom."

He had to laugh at that. "How could you? She's on your case all the time, following you around school, around practice and games, like you're the only thing in her life."

20

"Yeah, but it's not *me* she's interested in. It's my pulse, respiration, blood pressure. She doesn't even *know* me," Olivia finished, but there was not a tinge of self-pity in her words.

Walt pulled over to the side of the road and parked. "I find you very interesting," he said quietly. "I bet, if I got to know you better, I'd find you even more interesting." Their hands lay beside each other on the console between the two bucket seats. Walt had an uncontrollable urge to cover her small hand with his huge paw, but he didn't do it. He just stared at their hands, so close.

Olivia was very still, scarcely breathing. She'd been on dates with boys before, of course, but the guys she went out with were always more interested in themselves than her. Michael Barnes thought dating interfered with his goal of becoming a star cross-country runner, and eventually they split up when Olivia started feeling she was coming in a poor second. She never even felt comfortable with Jimmy Hilbert, who'd made such a fuss over her before she discovered he was going out with Nancy, too. With Walt, someone she knew, someone whose voice and hands and body were as familiar to her as the pendulum clock on her bedroom wall, she could almost relax.

"You sure don't say much, do you?" Walt chuckled.

"I was brought up to be super polite," Olivia said with a straight face. "I always let the other guy go first."

"Good. That gives me an opening for another

first." He bent toward her and she felt her own weight shifting, as if she was on the minitramp and about to lose her balance. But she could save herself from falling just by leaning slightly into his large, warm shoulder. He didn't touch her at all, not even a fingertip moved. But his lips were suddenly right next to her cheek, and she felt the cool whistle of his breath before the kiss. Then she turned awkwardly, not knowing what to do, and his mouth was too close to miss. She wished she had some lipstick because her lips were so dry. She didn't even have the chance to lick them before he kissed her, softly and hesitantly.

It was weird. This was Walt, not some strange person, not someone she'd dreamed about and hoped for. But it felt so good, so right. The only problem was, she didn't know what to do next. She didn't want the kiss to end, but she didn't want to seem mushy and emotional by kissing him back. They both hung there in midair, a little astounded at what had just taken place.

A car winging down the road saved them. The loud honk of the driver's horn made Walt and Olivia pull apart at the same time. Then they sat staring at each other, still too dumbfounded to speak.

"So. . . ." Walt cleared his throat. "Oh, boy."

She smiled into her scarf, the corners of her dark eyes crinkling happily as she reviewed the mysteries of the way she felt.

"Well, are you just going to sit there all day grinning like a loon?" he demanded.

"I might. Are you going to drive me home?"

"Sure." Well, that was it, then. He had failed miserably. Walt put the car in gear. Why was he such a dumb cluck? Why couldn't he leave well enough alone? They'd been having a perfectly nice conversation and then, he'd had to jump all over her. Why didn't girls put up signs when they wanted to be kissed? *I'm in the mood* or *Not today, thanks*.

Walt drove steadily around Narrow Brook Lake to the opposite side, near where Nancy lived. Still not a word from the small girl beside him. He plowed on down tree-lined roads to the newer houses, the ones away from the waterfront, which displayed their comfort and wealth in a less conspicuous way. He wasn't exactly sure where Olivia lived and didn't intend to ask. She'd have to speak first, even if it was just to give him directions.

"Next block, it's a right turn — number 33," she nearly whispered. And then she said, "But why don't you stop here so you can kiss me again?"

Angie had just taken the pile of mail off the front table and gone into the living room to sort it, when the phone rang. "Get it, will you, Al? I'm busy," she called, having discovered gold in the mass of bills and catalogs. A letter from Marc Filanno, from college!

"Hey, get the phone, will you, Andrew!" her older brother Al yelled to the next Poletti in line. It was a tradition that the youngest available got stuck with doing things his older siblings scorned.

"Get it yourself, stupid!" came the response from the kitchen.

She held the letter, savoring the neat writing on the envelope, the angle of the stamp, the postmark, the way the paper inside was folded. She was delirious with expectation, almost not daring to slit open the top — not because she worried that the reality would be less than perfect, but just because if she went ahead and read the letter, the ecstasy of waiting would be over.

Marc had graduated from high school last spring, and they'd gone out steadily over the summer. He had a job filling vending machines for some big company, and though the work was boring, it helped his family out with the college tuition. Now he was studying and working simultaneously, so Angie hadn't seen him in over a month. He'd been writing and calling regularly, and she got the impression that he hardly had time for anything.

"Andrew, get me a chicken leg or something would you?" Angie called into the kitchen. "That game gave me the most incredible appetite." Actually, it was the letter that made her hungry. Whenever she was really happy — which was most of the time — she ate. Angie loved to eat. She positively yearned for chocolate cake and double cheeseburgers with bacon. She liked to say that she could eat all day and actually *lose* weight from the exertion, but it wasn't true. She watched her weight like a hawk and was always rationing her treats — a skipped dessert today meant a sinful, gooey one tomorrow.

"Hey, Ange, I'm on the phone with that beautiful girl down the block. You'll have to starve," Andrew chuckled from the hallway, his hand over the receiver.

Angie took a breath and opened the letter, her eyes closed. She inhaled the very being of Marc from the page, thinking of his neat smile, the way his hair flopped over on one side, the way he kind of swayed when he walked. She opened her eyes and read:

Dear Angie,

I've thought long and hard about this, and believe me, I wouldn't write if I weren't absolutely sure that my decision is the best for both of us in the future. It may not look so hot to you now, but in a few months, you'll thank me.

I was talking to Elaine about this the other night, and she agreed that long-distance relationships are practically impossible, particularly when one person's in college and the other still has all those high school activities and concerns to worry about. It's really hard for two people in two such different worlds to make it click.

I'm always going to be fond of you, you know that, Angie, and even now, as I write this, I'm kicking myself for putting the damper on something that was so sweet, so special. But it's only natural that we all grow and change and experience different things

25

and different people. Please, don't sit around and moon over this — go out and cheer on that crowd the way you do so well. I'll always remember your sunny face.

Best,
Marc

"Who the hell's Elaine?" Angie whispered, but of course, she knew. Elaine was some sophisticated college girl who could probably discuss philosophy over a candlelight dinner and knew all the latest foreign films. She probably didn't even have to read the subtitles.

Angie was breathing very hard, all her feelings knotted up in one lump right under her chin. She couldn't cry — that was too dumb. She wanted to throw dishes at the wall, but that would be horribly wasteful. She was going to get control in a minute, in just a second, and as long as none of her brothers came in and started jabbering, she'd be fine.

The doorbell rang and she sat there, pinching the letter hard between two fingers, hoping she was hurting it.

"Ange, get the door, wouldya?" Andrew yelled. "I'm talking."

She didn't move and heard him curse, then put the phone down to see who was there. In less than a second, Nancy was in the room with her, breathless and excited.

"Well, I've located Pres and this is a perfect time for us to talk to him seriously about what happened at the game today. I saw his car parked

26

down by his uncle's house on my way back from Mary Ellen's, see, so if we go corner him there, he'll —" She took a good look at the normally bubbling-over-with-life girl slumped on the couch, gripping a piece of paper. "Oh, Angie, what's wrong?" She felt like a real dolt, to be babbling away when someone right in the same room with her was clearly about to commit suicide.

"If I said *nothing*, you wouldn't believe me, would you?" Angie was as close to tears as she'd been in a long time.

"No, I wouldn't." Nancy sat beside her, feeling the same sort of pain she'd experienced when Vanessa had been so mean to Mary Ellen. Why did she always have to have this awful empathy for everyone else? It was worse than when she went through it herself.

"Marc just sent me a 'Dear John' letter from college," Angie blurted out. "He — and somebody named Elaine — think we don't have anything in common anymore." And then the sobs came, loud and full. She couldn't stop herself; it was like something within her had broken and would never be mended. Even though she knew how useless it was to cry over a split boyfriend, it didn't stop the hurt. Why couldn't he have told her in person, for heaven's sake, or called, or done it gradually instead of all at once, so she could be prepared for it?

Nancy's arms were around her, and she felt an awkward patting on her right shoulder. She wished she could stop this stupid crying — she

27

wasn't really that tight with Nancy, and she felt so exposed.

"I know why he wants to split up, too. I really never thought it was that important to him. I mean, we were as good as married — everyone figured we'd end up together." She knotted her fist and pounded it into her thigh in frustration. "I should have gone to bed with him. Dumb, dumb, *dumb*. That's what guys want, isn't it? No matter how much they truly and sincerely love you, it's no good for them until you've done it. Right?" She turned to Nancy in a blind fury, the tears spilling everywhere.

"I don't think every single one of them is like that, Angie. And if it wasn't right for you —"

"No, it wasn't. He should have known that. We were going to wait, and he *said* that was fine. At least, most of the time, he did. I guess he didn't mean it. And then, this . . . this Elaine came along, and I guess he figured he didn't *have* to wait, so why should he?"

Nancy felt the ache in her own heart. She'd never been that close to a boy, really. Alex Hague had been the deepest relationship of her life, but he'd gone home to England. And then there was her romance with Ben Adamson, captain of Garrison High's basketball team. She'd been crazy about Ben, but that had been a wild, physical attraction more than anything else. He had epitomized sex to her. But dating someone from the enemy ranks was simply more than she could handle. Every time they went out, she'd be looking over her shoulder for Tarenton kids who might disapprove — and everyone did.

For a brief moment, she was jealous of Angie. What she'd had with Marc was really precious. But then, Nancy thought, what's the use if you have to go through all this pain at the end? Keep it light, keep it flirty, and you don't get hurt. You don't get the real highs, but you don't suffer the agonizing lows either. "Angie . . ." she begged.

"I'm all right now," Angie sniffed, holding back a second flow of tears that threatened to ruin all her good intentions. "Or at least I will be in a few decades."

"What a perfect louse," Nancy growled. "I don't know where guys get the idea that they can say, 'Poof, it's over,' and have it be over. It's like they think they're the only ones involved. You really cared about that nerd, too."

"I never felt about anyone the way I did about Marc." Angie sat there for a second, trying to be logical and sensible. Maybe that would stop the crying. "Do you think it could have been more being in love with just the *idea* of having a steady boyfriend? Like being in love with love? My mom always tells me she used to do that before she met my dad."

"Maybe. But what I saw when you were with Marc looked pretty real to me."

Angie's eyes filled again, and spilled over. She didn't want to do it, but she had no control over it. The letter lay, blotched with tears, in her lap.

"I have a box of tissues in my car," Nancy offered. "How about a drive? Just to get you out of the house for a while."

Angie nodded morosely. "If you like, we can

29

go see Pres. But you'll have to do the talking. I'm a hopeless case."

"You're a great and terrific person who has just been through the wringer," Nancy said fiercely, drawing Angie to her feet. "I want you to tell yourself that there's a lot in store for you, that this isn't the end of the world, not by a long shot."

Angie attempted to smile as she walked toward the door. She thought about being at the end of the world, a bleak place where you had to do trigonometry all day long and there was no rock music and no cheering. Where you'd never have to do your nails and hair before a date, because there were no dates.

Oh Marc, you left your mark on me, she thought glumly as she walked toward Nancy's car. Now how am I going to rub it out?

CHAPTER

3

It was five by the time Pres slammed on his brakes in front of James Tilford's house, the small but classy wood-and-glass structure on Beresford Road. The attached studio was hooked onto the back so inconspicuously you couldn't see it from the road. It was mostly skylights and high beams and it faced north — a perfect place for an artist.

"James, you there?" Pres called loudly as he knocked on the door. "It's me."

After a few seconds, the studio door swung open, revealing a small, wiry man with a salt-and-pepper beard, wearing baggy, paint-stained jeans and a T-shirt that was more holes than fabric. He had a pencil stuck behind his left ear, and his gray eyes were only half open, slitted in cynical appraisal of his nephew.

"Well, what little breeze blew you this way, old boy? Your dad want to convey some important message and wouldn't come in person?" James hadn't seen his brother in several years, by mutual agreement, as far as Pres could tell. An artist and a loner, divorced for the past ten years, James was something of a curiosity in Tarenton. He'd renounced his inheritance and decided to make it on his own, something Pres thought was totally commendable, if a little screwy, and something his father thought was grounds for commitment to a mental institution.

"James, I need a place to stay. How about it?" Pres rushed the words out as he stepped through the studio door. The roaring fire in the small wood stove that stood between two easels gave a cheery glow to the room.

"You and your dad have another fight?" James motioned Pres to a sitting cushion in the corner. The place had its own living area, a kitchen, and a bathroom.

"This time it was bad, man. I mean, I don't know how the two of us can even be related. He's totally anti everything I want to do, and I feel like I can't breathe in there anymore. It started with my cheerleading, and now it's —"

"With your *what*?" James guffawed. Then he saw the look on Pres's face. "Sorry, didn't mean to be such a critical boor. But are you pulling my leg? You're not really dancing around out there with the pompons, are you?"

Pres shrugged and decided not to push it. He hadn't talked to his uncle in a while, and maybe James had changed, too. Maybe he'd recently turned into another dictatorial grown-up, just disguised as a funky artist.

32

"Hey, it doesn't matter. I mean, it's lots of things, you know. The bottom line is that we don't get along. I'm old enough now, and I'm moving out. I just need a place to stay until I can find an apartment, okay? How about it?" This was the acid test. If James didn't ask too many questions, if he just let him be, Pres would know the guy was still okay.

James looked around the studio. "Well, it's humble, and it smells of turpentine, but it's yours if you want it. I'll be in and out of town for a couple of weeks, got a big group show coming up, so I'm not around that much."

"I can really stay?" Pres asked.

"Hey, I don't say what I don't mean." James dug in his pocket for a key, and threw it across the room to Pres. "Just a few house rules. Don't touch the work in progress upon pain of death, and if I catch you in here with drugs or booze or live-in women, you're out on your ear. Understand?"

"Sure, James," Pres's face lit up with gratitude. The guy was on his side! "And thanks, really. My father's going to have a fit when he finds out."

"It'll be good for him," James cackled.

"Say," Pres went on as his uncle started hauling a full crate of canvases toward the door, "is it okay if some of the girls from school come help me get settled? And help me with cooking and stuff?"

"As long as there's no funny business on my property, it's cool. You're young and tender and I don't want to be responsible for your ultimate destruction." He rolled his eyes evilly and tried to twirl his tiny mustache like the villain in a melodrama.

Pres had to laugh at his uncle. The guy was weird, no doubt about it. But at least he could see somebody else's point of view. "You're on. And thanks again," he said as his uncle vanished, hidden behind a large red painting.

Pres looked around, and the thought suddenly dawned on him that he didn't have to be home in time for dinner. With a whoop of delight, he tossed the key in the air. His key to freedom.

Mary Ellen ran toward the gym Monday afternoon, certain that she was going to be late to practice. The halls were practically deserted as she raced along. The only sound was that of her rundown heels on the marble beneath her. If there was one thing Ardith wouldn't tolerate, it was kids who didn't come in on time. To her, it was a sign of not caring enough. That was one thing that couldn't be said about Mary Ellen — she certainly cared. More than anything, probably, except getting out of Tarenton, moving to New York, and making it big.

"You're always in such a hurry. You're going to miss an awful lot if you keep rushing, sweetheart."

Mary Ellen's face flushed, and she didn't have to look up to know that it was Patrick. He had this way of confronting her, of looming over her so large he blotted out everything else in her mind. All she could think about when he was close to her was her body and his, their mouths pressed close in a kiss, his powerful arms drawing

34

her into an embrace from which she never wanted to be released. It was all she could do to keep herself from touching him.

"I'm late for practice." She took just one look up into his deep brown eyes and she was lost, gone, out to lunch for the duration. What was it about him that turned her on this way? He wasn't conventionally handsome, but that wide smile held so much promise, those eyes drew her like a magnet, and that body. . . . It was just sex, she knew that, and she could get over it if she tried, but despite her best intentions, it seemed to get harder and harder.

"You're better than the rest of them — you don't need as much practice. In some other areas, however, you could use a little extra work." And with that, he took her books out of her arms and replaced them with his own massive frame. Bending over her, he smoothed the hair off her forehead, then gently kissed the soft white skin. She closed her eyes, willing herself not to respond. She had the oddest feeling, as if her knees were going to give. She wanted to throw her arms around him, crush him to her, but something inside screamed, *No!* It was too dangerous, practically lethal. Even as his lips moved along the side of her cheek and down to her eager mouth, she started pulling away. This was so wrong!

The more she kissed Patrick, the closer they'd be, and soon the world would acknowledge that they were a couple. *Bus Driver's Daughter To Wed Trash Collector* — she could see the headline now. The only way she'd get to New York would be on their honeymoon. They'd see the sights and take pictures for their scrapbook and then, before she knew it, they'd be back in Tarenton, home sweet home. And then, babies. Her figure and looks would vanish before she was twenty-five.

The scenario scared her so much she literally wrenched herself out of his arms, grabbing her books and mumbling something about seeing him later but she really had to run. She was nearly free and clear, nearly out of his magnetic field, when someone else came around the bend of the hallway. Vanessa.

"Wow, guess I just missed some hot action, huh?" she smirked. "Between you two and Pres and Kerry right down the hall, this school is a regular Love Boat. It's so heartwarming to see two young hearts beating as one." She batted her heavily mascaraed eyelashes so hard they looked as if they were going to break off.

"*Can* it, Vanessa." Patrick stalked away from her as though she had a disease. Mary Ellen had already fled, nearly colliding with Pres and Kerry as she skidded toward the gym door. The two of them weren't looking particularly lovey-dovey, but rather worried and scared, Mary Ellen noticed. Kerry, a sophomore with an open personality and the sweet, soft face of an angel, was looking up at Pres adoringly.

"Oh, great, we can both get some demerits." Pres laughed as he saw Mary Ellen, trying to cover up his real mood. "You sure you don't mind waiting for me, Kerry?" he asked in a different tone, touching her arm.

36

"Of course not. I'll be in the library. You two better hurry." She smiled warmly at Mary Ellen, who couldn't help but marvel at the younger girl's goodness. She was just so *nice* — not Pres's type at all. It was hard for everyone to believe that he'd stopped playing the field for this rather plump, kind of lackluster girl. But when he looked at her, she blossomed.

"Mrs. Engborg's going to kill us, but at least she'll demolish you first, because of Saturday's game," Mary Ellen muttered as they hurried into the gym together.

"That means you get to watch me suffer before your own execution. Could be a gruesome sight." Pres smiled wickedly, ushering her gallantly ahead of him.

"Well, how kind of you two to join us," Ardith Engborg said in a deadly calm voice. "I don't suppose you feel you've missed anything, so if you'll consent to changing into your practice clothes, we'll go right on from where we are. Angie, try that C-jump again. And higher this time. Walt, this is not amateur hour — I expect some real action from all of you."

As Mary Ellen threw off her clothes in the locker room, she was struck by the fact that she felt more energetic than she had in a long time. Usually, when Vanessa got after her and Ardith was on her case, she couldn't help sulking. Today, though, it was different. She was a fireball; she wanted to get out there and lead the others on to glory. She tied her shining blonde hair into a ponytail and fluffed out the little tendrils on the side, strangely impressed with the vision she

37

saw in the mirror. No matter that her practice clothes were old and faded from dozens of washings. She felt good — she actually felt rich!

She practically skipped back into the gym and was smiling until she realized why she felt so good. It was Patrick, his hands on her, his overwhelming presence. His love made her shine. And that was enough to send her spirits reeling back down into the lower depths. Oh, no, she thought as she took her place between Nancy and Olivia for the Tiger cheer. I can't do this to myself — I can't. Starting today, I'll try to stay away from him entirely. No more kisses, no more. It's me and Donny, period. But as she jumped and leapt around the floor, there was Patrick, his wonderful image swimming before her very eyes.

"We got the talent, we got the team,
Watch us now — see what we mean.
There's no limit to our spirit,
We're gonna win 'cause we're really in it!"

Angie tried for a triple roll to coincide with Olivia's, but the two girls collided in space, landing hard on the mat.

"Hey, watch where you're going, will you?" Angie kept trying to concentrate, but it was impossible. There was Marc, of course. One minute she wanted to get him on the phone and scream at him; the next, she was filled with an overwhelming desire to call and beg him to come back to her. And then there was Pres — and what she and Nancy had learned on Saturday

38

afternoon. They'd kept their mouths shut till now, but eventually, the news would be out. She felt funny about knowing it first and not being able to tell.

"You watch it — I was right in place," Olivia huffed, looking to Walt for support. He'd called her on Sunday, just to chat. She'd half expected him to ask her out, but maybe he was just too shy. Anyway, she wasn't going to push — she could wait. In the meantime, this was just fine.

"Stop bickering, you two." Ardith put her hands on her narrow hips and motioned them to the center of the floor. She had on a lavender leotard under a plum-colored jumpsuit, with black leg warmers, and in her current state of mind she seemed very much like an angry, thin bunch of grapes.

"Sit down, everybody. I don't know what's going on here, but it has to stop. I'm going to give you all a chance to speak up, and then we'll get back to work. And I *mean* work! Not this halfhearted attempt at running around like chickens without heads." She did a neat Turk sit and motioned them to join her. "Okay, let's go around in a circle. Pres, you want to talk about Saturday?"

"No," he answered curtly.

Ardith's eyes narrowed. "Anyone else care to shed some light on Pres's problems?"

Nancy and Angie exchanged furtive glances, and shifted uncomfortably. That was pretty lousy, asking them to rat on a team member. Ardith didn't usually do things like this, but she was clearly upset.

39

"Gee, you're not your usual talkative selves, are you?" she stated sarcastically. "Olivia, why don't you break the ice?"

Olivia, seated next to Walt, just bit her lips and crossed her arms. Walt glanced down at her protectively.

"I think we should get back to work," Mary Ellen offered. "We'll try harder — how about that, Mrs. Engborg?" She bounded up, willing herself to have enough spirit for the whole team. The others straggled to their feet, embarrassed, and eager to get off the hook. There were just some things you didn't tell adults.

"Well, *work*, then," their leader huffed in disgust. "Pres, I want to see you tomorrow in my office, eight-thirty sharp. Is that clear?"

"Very." His tone wasn't sullen or rude, but it wasn't compliant either.

And then they got down to it, pacing through routines until their clothes were soaked with sweat and their limbs ached. They practiced rolls and leaps, carries and lifts; they did enough walkovers and back flips to induce stomach cramps — but nobody complained. Like machines, they worked silently and efficiently, each lost in a quiet physical world where everything else faded into the background. Nothing counted but the grueling, agonizing work.

They were dismissed at six, and Pres raced through his shower, on his way out of the locker room before Walt had even peeled off his soaking sweats. Pres's body was tired, but he was better now than he'd been in a long time. So Ardith would chew him out tomorrow — so what? He could take anything.

"You okay?" Walt stood in front of the shower stall naked, a towel around his muscular neck.

"Hey, I'm cool, man. Don't let it worry you." He was out the door and down the hall without waiting for a response, thinking about the evening to come, about that little studio, and a nice fire, and maybe a frozen TV dinner. There she was. There was Kerry, just where she said she'd be, in front of the library door, her silvery jacket with its thin lavender strip across the yoke slung over her shoulder.

"They closed up a few minutes ago," she explained as he kissed her lightly and led the way down the stairs, toward the front door of Tarenton High. "You look beat."

"Sort of." He smiled down into her clear, brown eyes, so caring and trusting. Having Kerry around was a balm on the wound of all that had happened to him in the past few days. "Grocery shopping first, okay? You have to tell me what to buy."

She grinned, her round face lighting up. "I made a list after I finished my French vocabulary. Real healthy stuff — I hope you can take it."

"Baby, I can take it if you can." They started laughing and didn't stop until they were outside in the parking lot. The cars of the people on the team and those of a few faculty members were the only ones left. It was starting to get dark.

As Pres opened the door of his Porsche for her,

Kerry turned to him, a look of deep concern furrowing her brow. "Hey, what about this? How about if you just stop off at home and let them know where you're living? That wouldn't be so hard, would it?"

He sighed and was about to answer, when a husky voice spoke up, startling them both. "You mean you haven't told *them*? Oh, Pres, how cruel of you." Vanessa had been sitting on top of a Toyota right beside them, and they hadn't even seen her. She was like the wicked witch in a fairy tale, popping up when you least expected her.

"What do you know about it?" He peered at her suspiciously. Pres had dated Vanessa off and on for the past year. He had to admit she turned him on. She was always so willing. But he could anticipate most of her fast moves by now. He was one of the only people she couldn't con — possibly because he had a lot of the same instincts about dealing with life that she did. What saved him was that he generally used his better judgment and most of the time, he didn't stoop to being a louse.

"I just couldn't help overhearing you two chatting in the hall before practice," she shrugged casually. The wind blew her thick ebony hair out, fanlike, and picked up the collar on her loden green coat. She drew it closer around her as she smiled at Pres, running her tongue over her lips, relishing the sound of her own words. "So you moved out. You're cutting the apron strings. Bully for you. Actually, I have my eye on a place of my own for this summer. It's simply perfect. You'd love it, darling." She put a kid-gloved hand on his arm. He shook it off, but her words brought definite pictures to his mind.

"Let's get going, Kerry." He determinedly opened the door for her and, without even a backward glance at Vanessa, Kerry climbed inside. She still had trouble believing that she was dating Pres Tilford, that he liked her as much as she did him, that he wanted to hold her and kiss her and be with her. So when something like this happened, when a verbal duel was going on right in front of her, she figured the smartest thing to do was shut up and act as if she wasn't there.

"How about a lift, Pres? My dad's late tonight," Vanessa flirted. "The three of us would probably fit, if Kerry squeezed those nice round thighs in a little. You don't mind, do you, dear?"

"I. . . ." The younger girl, huddled in her silver jacket, thought it was unkind and unfair of Vanessa to discuss her weight. But she was simply not in Vanessa's league and couldn't begin to think of a suitable comeback.

"Forget it, Vannie. Not tonight." Pres walked around to the driver's side.

But Vanessa wasn't phased in the least, even though Pres had used her most-hated nickname. She stood calmly, hiding the fact that her brain was working overtime. "Kerry, do you know we all used to call your boyfriend Presto Chango? That's because he was out with a different girl practically every night. Isn't it true, Presto?"

"We better get going, Pres," Kerry said uneasily, "if we're going to make all those stops and do all those errands."

"Vanessa, you ever hear the one about sticks and stones? Names will never hurt me."

"No, of course not, Presto. But moving out of your parents' house could do some irreparable damage, couldn't it? I was just thinking — it might get you kicked off the team."

"What are you talking about?" He slammed his door and came back around to her, grabbing her by the arm.

"I'm sure my daddy knows some rule about high school kids living in proper settings." She bent down casually, giving a tug to her polished boots.

"What do you want, anyway? What's in it for you?" Pres demanded in a hushed whisper, so low that Kerry couldn't hear.

Vanessa smiled, her hot-pink lips inviting and threatening at the same time. "Well, for one thing, Presto, I want *you*. And for another, I just never believed that boys really belonged on the field or the court, unless they were in the game. They look weird jumping around, doing all those acrobatics. I mean, imagine telling somebody your boyfriend is a cheerleader. It's tacky."

"Well, I'm sorry to make things tough for you, but *I'm* going to tell everyone, so you don't have to. I'm living with my uncle, and that's got to be a perfectly all right arrangement. So don't get your hopes up, Vannie." He stalked around the car, threw himself into the driver's seat, and turned the key hard in the ignition. The Porsche pulled out like a beast that had just been released from its cage.

"Take it easy," Kerry .pleaded. "I don't care

44

what that girl says. It's dumb. All I care about is you."

Pres let up his pressure on the gas pedal slightly and glanced over at her. "You're a sweetheart. Hey, you know she was lying, don't you?"

"I know what I see and feel." Kerry settled back in her seat, running her hands through her flyaway hair. "Now tell me, how do you feel about fish for dinner?"

"Fish?! Are you kidding! Fish is one of the things I left home to get away from."

Kerry giggled, and her laugh lifted his mood. "But it's brain food, Pres. You'll think better."

"Tell me about it." And yet, as they drove along, it occurred to him that he was going to have to do a lot of fast thinking tomorrow when Ardith confronted him. And once he'd told the truth, once she knew what was bugging him, what was he going to do then?

CHAPTER

Pres didn't sleep very well. After Kerry had cooked the fish for an an hour, they'd discovered that it was more inedible than it normally would have been, so they scrapped it and ate chips with their Cokes instead. Then, because she had to be home by nine on weeknights, they'd driven back to her place, and after that, he'd been alone — by himself in a strange, unfriendly place.

He mooned around the studio, wondering why James didn't have a TV, wondering what Ardith was going to do to him, wondering (only once or twice) what his parents were thinking. Then he'd opened up the sleeper-sofa and plopped down on it, willing sleep to come. He was drowsy one minute and wide awake the next. Finally, the fire went out and he huddled in the thermal blanket for the rest of the night.

There were only a few cars in the parking lot when he pulled the Porsche into his favorite spot under a large spreading maple, now bare and majestic in the morning sun. He noticed Vanessa's father's car — that guy was always up at the crack of dawn to do his laps around the track. He tried to get his daughter to join him, but she hated any kind of exercise where you couldn't show off in front of other people. Jogging was much too solitary an activity for somebody as flashy as Vanessa.

But Pres was surprised to see Vanessa standing in front of the principal's office, as he walked into the front hall of Tarenton High. She looked very pleased with herself, not like she was about to be chewed out. He was immediately suspicious. Vanessa just oozed trouble — and if it wasn't around, she'd make it. He shouldered his way down the corridor just as the principal's door opened and Mrs. Oetjen ushered Vanessa inside.

"That girl deserves twenty to life for making people miserable," he muttered to himself on his way up to Ardith's office. Down the hall, silhouetted against the glass, he could see his coach's diminutive form pacing back and forth in the tiny room. He took a deep breath and approached her inner sanctum. Then he knocked once and opened the door.

"You didn't have to pick me up." Olivia grinned happily, settling back in the seat of Walt's Jeep with a look of total satisfaction on her face.

"You're absolutely right. Want to get out and walk?" He kept his eyes on the road, but he might as well have been staring deep into Olivia's

47

for all the attention he was paying to the other drivers around him.

"Hmm. Well, since you went to all the trouble of getting to my house so early, and since you had to get the third degree from my mother, I guess I'll stick around. Hey, watch that pothole!"

The two of them bounced in the air as the Jeep veered to the right just a bit too fast.

"That was not a third degree," Walt protested as he got back in line with the other drivers. "That was a fourth, fifth, and tenth degree rolled into one. Boy, I try to think nice thoughts about most people's parents most of the time, but Livvy, it's hard with her. What did she mean about my intellectual potential, anyway?"

"Oh, if you don't have an IQ of 947, there's clearly something wrong with you," Olivia giggled. "Not to mention your health, your looks, your moral character, and all your ancestors back to year one — and their health."

"Well, I do have a sense of humor," he said. "Is that on her list?"

"Nope. Unimportant."

"How about my charming personality?"

"No good."

"How about my phenomenal gymnastic ability?"

"Absolutely no points." Olivia gave him the thumbs-down sign.

"How about a date?" Walt said softly. "Like a movie and a burger after? Or a burger and a movie? Or two burgers and two movies?" He pulled into the school parking lot and looked at her eagerly. It was really difficult for him to just blurt things out like that.

"I'd love to." Olivia looked at him with shining eyes. "Anytime," she added, deciding that she would make it easier for him.

"Tomorrow night," he said, helping her down from the high seat. Her hand was warm and it fit perfectly in his. "So you'll have time to go through the shopping list with your mom."

They were both laughing as they walked into the hall and passed Nancy on her way to first-period math. She looked at them, then did a double take. They could tell she was trying to put some pieces together.

"Good morning, guys," she said cheerfully.

"Hi, yourself," Walt practically sang. He would have given a cheer right there in the crowded first-floor corridor if Vanessa hadn't at that moment walked out of Mrs. Oetjen's office, with the principal's arm around her shoulder. The very sight made him itch all over.

"Look who's just polished up an apple for the teacher," he said to the girls under his breath. "Now what's she up to?"

He didn't have to ask because Vanessa was only too delighted to tell. As soon as Mrs. Oetjen had turned around, the girl was rushing over to them, eager to spread her bad news as fast as possible.

"Well, it's finally happened," she began by way of greeting. "You kids are in for a real surprise. Nancy, where *did* you get that darling hat? It makes you look so . . . sweet," she growled.

"What's happened, Vanessa?" Walt demanded. "Don't tell me you're going to fulfill our wildest dreams and move to Outer Mongolia?"

She didn't smile, didn't even bother to acknowledge his remark. "Pres is off the cheerleading squad. He's on probation," she announced, "which puts all of you in a rather big pickle, doesn't it?" And with that she flounced away.

"*What* did she mean by that?" Olivia screwed up her face in annoyance. Walt just shrugged, but Nancy had one hand pressed over her eyes.

"What do you know about this?" Olivia asked when Nancy made a strange little noise way back in her throat.

"I can guess what Vanessa was discussing with Mrs. Oetjen," she said slowly. "I suppose you guys may as well know. Angie and I have been busting to tell someone since Saturday. And if everybody already knows. . . ." She thought about it for a second, then took a deep breath and spilled the beans.

"Mrs. Engborg, listen, I'm under perfectly good supervision. My Uncle James is just as much a parental authority as my parents. More — he actually cares what happens to me." Pres laughed disparagingly.

"I'm very sorry, Pres, but this is out of my control." The coach looked very businesslike and solemn. "There happens to be a school rule. Unless a student's parents have split up or there's a death in a family or there's some extenuating circumstance that would make regular family life impossible, you have to be living at home.

50

You cannot pick up and leave just because it suits you."

"But I've got a home. My uncle's practically a live-in chaperone," he lied. Technically, he'd only seen James once since Saturday.

"I'm not going to argue," Ardith said firmly. "Not living at home means probation. Probation means no extracurriculars. And that means you're off the team."

His face was stricken. Of course, somewhere, deep down, he'd expected this. When Vanessa had brought it up, he'd had some wacko hope that he could wangle his way around any rule. But now he'd have to face the responsibilities of moving out, and getting bumped from cheerleading was just one of them. Fleetingly, it occurred to him that he'd only tried out for the team to spite his father, so now it didn't really matter. But the point was, *now* cheering was a big part of his life.

"Ardith," he began, just as her office door opened. Mrs. Oetjen was standing there.

"You've told him." She stated this — didn't ask it.

"Yes, he knows," Ardith said. But she turned back to Pres with a softer expression on her face. "How about you solving this problem for everybody, Pres?" she asked rather kindly. "You've made your point, so now you can get on with life. All you have to do is move back home and the restriction will be withdrawn. Isn't that true, Mrs. Oetjen?"

The principal hesitated a moment, then nodded. "I suppose that would be acceptable."

Pres's mouth curved upward in a half smile that was vaguely reminiscent of his father's. "Not on a bet," he murmured. "I didn't do it just to prove something. I did it because I had to, don't you see? I was going nuts in that house."

"We could all see that your work has been suffering," Ardith acknowledged. "But this doesn't help matters. Pres, you know as well as I do — and the rest of the kids on the team know, too — that you're preoccupied and lacking in concentration. Nothing you do has the same energy or enthusiasm as before. And then there was the incident at Saturday's game. If you're capable of dropping a girl during a cheer, you're jeopardizing the whole squad, don't you see? As long as you persist in this self-centered behavior, you can't be a team member."

The principal walked inside and sat down in Ardith's second chair, facing Pres with a look of desperation on her face. "Your parents are extremely concerned, as you may well imagine. They'd do anything to have you come back."

For a second, Pres's cockiness faded. "You mean, they called you?"

"Well, naturally. They wanted to know if you'd turned up in school yesterday. When I assured them you were here, they seemed rather surprised, but pleased. At that point, they begged me not to tell anyone, which is why Mrs. Engborg didn't know at your practice in the afternoon. I take it they've been talking to your uncle every day, without satisfaction."

Pres started to laugh. It began as a snort and amplified to a roar. The tiny office shook with his sound. The two women glared at him, incredulous. "Don't you see?" he gasped when he finally caught his breath. "This is exactly what's so screwy! They never talk to *me* — *never*. They go to everybody else and talk *about* me! Geez." He thought about the phone in Uncle James's studio, how he'd sat next to it for an hour the previous night, hoping it would ring.

"They are clearly having some difficulties expressing themselves, Pres, but perhaps, you would, too, if you were the stricken parent instead of the rebellious child."

He stood up, his shoulders squared off as if for battle. "Well, I'm not giving in or giving up. You can do whatever you want to me. I have a place to stay and it suits me fine. And as for cheerleading," he spat the word at Ardith, "you can get yourself another guy. Because I don't need it — or you." With that, he stomped out, feeling a lot less sure of himself than he wanted to. He'd be late to math on top of everything — what a bummer. His only satisfaction right now was in imagining how burned his father must be. What he wouldn't give to see the look on Preston Tilford II's face!

Donny Parrish followed Mary Ellen down the cafeteria line, picking dishes at random. He was too busy staring at the luscious long legs in front of him, admiring the way they neatly curved upward to the thighs and small of her back. Mary Ellen sure was something! And that hair — long silk he could run his fingers through endlessly, perfect strands that curled around his giant hands whenever he wanted them to. Yeah, come to think of it, he was a lucky guy. Dating a girl who wasn't only gorgeous, but who really had it together. Sometimes she was a little hard to handle, because she always expected more than she got, but he was used to her moods by now. They were kind of cute, in a way.

"Say, you must be starving." Mary Ellen laughed, her brilliant smile gleaming at him.

"Huh?" Donny snapped out of his trance and looked directly at her. "What do you mean?"

"I know being the captain of Tarenton's basketball team is a huge job and you work up a terrible appetite and everything, but *four* ham and cheese sandwiches for lunch on top of chili seems like overkill to me."

"Oh, yeah. I forgot. Must be a little fever left from my flu or something." He quickly put three of the sandwiches back, feeling dumb and embarrassed. He hated being shown up — it just wasn't right for someone to point out his mistakes — even if it was Mary Ellen, the most desirable girl in school doing it.

Mary Ellen had only picked a salad herself. Dieting had nothing to do with her choice — the problem was financial. Of course she brown-bagged it every day, to save money, but when Donny asked her to eat lunch with him, she simply couldn't drag out a homemade peanut butter and jelly and eat it with any kind of grace. So she'd scrimp on something else that week.

As they walked to the cashier's station and paid, Mary Ellen caught a glimpse of a dark head at the other end of the line. Her face turned red as he spotted her, Patrick! *Oh please*, she prayed silently, *let him just leave us alone. I can't deal with him and Donny at the same time.*

But of course, as soon as they had found their seats and Donny had gallantly pulled out a chair for her, nuzzling her neck and shoulders as he sat beside her, Patrick went into action. Leaving his tray with the cashier, he took a high-flying leap in the air and hurdled the counter, landing on both knees only inches from Mary Ellen. As the kids around them cheered at his acrobatic antics, he steadied himself with a hand on her leg. She reacted immediately when he touched her.

"This seat taken?" he asked Donny casually with a wink up at Mary Ellen.

Donny weighed the alternatives before speaking. "Well, actually, some of the guys from the team said they'd join us. . . ."

"They're not here yet, though. Guess it'll be okay. I'll eat fast. I'm not that hungry today — for *food*, that is," he added meaningfully to Mary Ellen.

Donny shrugged angrily and turned to his chili, as Patrick went to retrieve his tray.

"Donny," Mary Ellen said quickly, "he doesn't have to eat with us, you know. Just tell him to get lost."

"Well, why don't *you* tell him?" Donny asked brusquely, his wholesome, all-American face suddenly turning mean. "You're the one who knows him so well."

"Donny, you sound like you're jealous," Mary Ellen forced a casual laugh. "And that's perfectly ridiculous." She was lying, of course. Donny's jealousy was perfectly justified. All Patrick had to do was sit down next to her and her stomach would whirl around like a top. She dug into her salad, hoping to be finished by the time Patrick got back.

But it was Walt and Angie who made it to their table first, with Olivia bringing up the rear. The three of them looked like survivors of a shipwreck.

"Can we sit down?" Angie asked hopelessly, taking the chair Patrick had reserved without waiting for a response.

Walt nodded a perfunctory hello to Donny, then took two chairs for Olivia and himself. "Nancy's coming over later. She had a hot and heavy session with a frog in bio lab. Right before lunch, too. Yuk." He wrinkled his nose.

"Cut the jokes, Walt." Angie just kept looking at Mary Ellen as if she was about to burst into tears.

"What *is* it with all of you?" Mary Ellen put down her fork, suddenly forgetting about Donny and Patrick and her elaborate juggling act with the two of them.

"I knew she hadn't heard yet," Olivia sighed.

"It's bad, Melon," Angie shook her head, forgetting how much Mary Ellen hated that nickname. "But I better just blurt it out. Pres has been kicked off the cheerleading squad, as of this morning. It's official."

"You're crazy!" Mary Ellen looked at each one of them, but their eyes all said the same thing.

"What's going on?" Donny asked eagerly, but

56

no one paid the slightest attention to him.

"Yeah, what *is* going on?" Patrick asked as he strode back toward them with his tray, and squeezed a chair in between Olivia and Mary Ellen. He was so close, their knees bumped under the table. "All of you look like death warmed over."

"You remember how awful Pres was at the game Saturday," Olivia went on to Mary Ellen, completely ignoring Patrick as well as Donny. "Turns out he was going through some real hard times at home, so he just moved out. His uncle has some studio he's staying in, but he's not supposed to, according to school rules. So Mrs. Oetjen put him on probation until he moves back home."

"Which, rumor has it, he's not about to do," Walt continued. "He was pretty hard on Ardith — told her to look for some other cheerleader. He never was awfully gung ho about getting on the team. Remember how I had to pressure him into it?"

Mary Ellen sat there stunned, hardly moving, as the information sank in. She was ashamed to realize that her first reaction was annoyance that she hadn't found out first. After all, she was the captain of the squad. And on top of that, she'd dated Pres. Why couldn't he have told her? That little Kerry must know, she thought suddenly, recalling the scene outside the gym the previous night. That's what they were talking about! That's why they looked so worried.

"Well, what are we going to do?" she asked at last. "It's absurd to think that some other guy could take over for Pres at this stage. I mean, we've got one game this weekend, and from then on till the end of the season we're booked solid. How can somebody come in cold and learn all our routines?"

Donny, feeling totally left out, decided to contribute something to the conversation. "Aw, it's not like putting in a new shooter on the basketball team. Anyone can learn a few high kicks and cheers."

The other four just glared at him. Patrick laughed aloud. "Oh, boy, you've done it now!" he guffawed at the basketball star. He turned to Mary Ellen. "I think you should lodge a protest with Mrs. Oetjen and get Pres back."

"Olivia and I already tried that, Patrick," Walt sighed. "Talking to that woman is like talking to a rock."

"Oh, how could Pres *do* this to us!" Angie wailed as Nancy walked over, looking as grim as the rest of them. She was holding her food tray at arm's length from her body.

"Well, at last! There you are," Walt nodded, pulling over a chair for her. "Why are you holding your tray like that?"

"Because I stink of embalmed frog, that's why. I don't want to get too close. I've washed my hands three times, and I still feel that slime. One of you is going to have to feed me so I don't get my hands near my mouth. What have we decided about Pres?" she asked in the same breath.

Donny made a big show of pushing back his chair and clearing his throat. "I'm done with lunch, Mary Ellen, and since you're so busy over here, I think I'll take a walk. See you later, okay?" He stood there for a minute, hoping she'd tell him to stay, hoping Patrick would take the hint and leave, but all he got was a shrug.

"Sure. Later, Donny." She couldn't be bothered keeping up a front, couldn't even bother to smile.

As soon as Donny'd walked over to the tray return, Mary Ellen felt Patrick's arm slip around her. "Hey, it's not so bad," he whispered soothingly in her ear. "You kids are wonderful at improvising things. Just cut out all Pres's parts and work around the holes. It'll look great — you'll see."

"It'll look dumb!" Angie proclaimed. "He does all the big lifts! It's all coordinated, don't you see? And we're going to look really awful, going up against Muskeagtown's Twinkling Twelve on Saturday, staggering around like we don't know what's what."

Muskeagtown's twelve Varsity cheerleaders were something to see. They had a graceful, ballet style that caught the eye and flowed like honey over a crowd. Mary Ellen had to admit Angie was right. Five of them improvising against the Muskeagtown squad doing their finely honed steps would spell disaster.

"All right, listen, here's the plan. We'll find a new guy. The school is full of guys who want to fool around with four girls." Mary Ellen said firmly. "A couple of us will work with him every minute, day and night. We'll drill him till he's perfect. But Ardith's going to have to make it clear to him that he's only a temp. In the mean-

59

time, the rest of us will work on Pres. He's got to come back," she said despairingly, not really knowing whether she wanted him back because he was good for the team or because someday, somehow, he might be good for her.

She hadn't given up hope that one day their relationship would really click and together, they'd waltz off out of this podunk town forever. Pres had it all: looks, brains, wealth, and the proper attitude about taking what was his from life. Moving out on his folks proved that beyond a doubt.

"Well, we'll try it." Walt nodded, getting up as the next bell rang and everyone started for the tray return. "But we're going to need an awful lot of luck to get by this Saturday."

"I'm willing to work hard if you can find another guy who is, too," Olivia said staunchly.

"Me, too," Nancy agreed.

"Hey," Angie said softly. They all stopped where they were and looked at her. "What about Pres? He must be feeling absolutely awful." She couldn't help but relate to this. She was still seeing Marc everywhere, hearing his voice, smelling his clean, starched shirts, no matter how hard she tried to concentrate on forgetting him. She knew all too well how personal problems could blot out everything else in life.

"Pres is tough," Patrick assured her, his hand reaching for Mary Ellen's as they started out the cafeteria door. "He'll get by."

"We'll all get by," Angie agreed. "The question is, what'll it cost us?"

No one had an answer for that.

CHAPTER 5

Five rather disgruntled cheerleaders lay sprawled on the gym mats, waiting. Ardith usually beat them to it, and was generally warming up as they arrived, but today she was closeted in her office, and there was someone in there with her. The new guy, whom she had found.

"Did you see Pres today?" Angie stretched her long, lean legs out on the floor in front of her, pulling down the bottoms of her forest green sweat pants. "He hardly even nodded at me when I passed him in the hall this afternoon. He looks just awful."

"Mr. Sanders called on him in history and he drew a blank," Nancy offered. "Either that, or he was thinking of something else."

"How could he not be?" Mary Ellen demanded. Her hair was done in intricate braids, overlapping and crisscrossing on top of her head. That generally made her feel queenlike, but today, her head felt heavy and overloaded. Whether it was the braids or her thoughts, she didn't feel up to a strenuous practice. "I don't know — this whole thing is a terrible mess."

"The only thing worse is if Ardith decides to replace Pres with Vanessa," Nancy muttered. "Seeing as how she knows all the cheers already, I mean."

"But . . . oh, come *on!*" Walt practically yelled. "It's gonna be a guy. She couldn't do that to us — she wouldn't!"

"She wouldn't do it to herself," Angie giggled. "I think Ardith hates Vanessa almost as much as we do."

But there was no more time for gossip, because the coach's door opened and she marched out briskly, her maroon, velour sweat suit a beacon in the tan and gray gym. Behind her was a kid about her size with a mop of curly black hair and prominent high cheekbones, above which black eyes looked wary and cautious.

"Oh, no!" Nancy shut her eyes tight and hugged her knees to her chest. "Not him. Why did it have to be him?"

"Who is he?" Walt whispered.

"Guys, this is Josh Breitman," Ardith volunteered. "I guess you all know each other, at least by sight. Josh is a senior, a very fine gymnast, and a really quick study," Ardith rushed on. "He understands that we've got an emergency here, and he's willing to give his all to work with us. He feels sure he'll be ready by Saturday's game, and I have complete confidence in him." She glared at them all. "That means I have confidence

62

in you five to make things easier for him."

"Hi, everyone." Josh's voice was extremely deep, a rumble that came from down in his chest. "Hi, Nancy. How're you doing?"

Nancy just nodded. She looked as if someone had just stepped on her toes during a routine. Angie gave her a nudge in the ribs, but she didn't respond.

"So, let's get going," Ardith suggested. "Mary Ellen, would you please start the warm-up. And talk as you go — I want Josh to get everything the first time, if possible." She took a seat facing them on the mat that lay in front of the mirror. The others straggled to their feet and took their places in front of her. She reached over and turned on the tape recorder. A Stones number blasted off the gym walls.

"Okay," Mary Ellen willed herself to seem enthusiastic and energetic, but she couldn't stop thinking about Pres. He should have been there with them. He should have at least sought them out earlier in the day to talk about things. But that was Pres all over — he had to be himself, and insist he was right about it at the same time.

"Arms overhead, and swing your torso, right and left and keep it going!" she shouted, her mind a zillion miles away. Luckily, she knew the warm-up so well she didn't have to think about it. Her hips and torso swung and swiveled, her toes arched and flexed on command. While her body worked, the rest of her was free to consider what she really wanted to do about this lousy situation. As captain of the squad, she felt it was her duty to get things back in shape. Of course, she had to admit to herself as she caught a glimpse of Josh working behind her in the mirror, he was pretty good. Nice relaxed movements, good tempo, and a smile on his face. But what was Nancy all bummed out about? She looked as if she'd rather be doing calculus.

"Walt, you take over," Ardith said after about twenty minutes, when all the kids were sweating profusely. "Let's work on the minitramp for a while, get in some jumps and leaps. From there, we'll go to ground work and do cartwheels and walkovers. Josh, you shouldn't have any trouble with this part — it's just like gymnastics class."

"Sure, Mrs. Engborg. No problem," he said confidently.

Walt led the group in a series of increasingly complex maneuvers on the minitramp, stuff that was easy for him and Olivia, the most athletic of the team. Mary Ellen and Angie, although not naturally adapted to difficult moves, performed them flawlessly because of their years of practice. Only Nancy still had trouble with this part of the workout, and today her faults seemed magnified ten times over. When she missed her third doubleback somersault on the tramp, it was Josh who stopped the next person in line from going on.

"Ah, do you mind if I just give you a couple of pointers, Nance? If you spot on that wall over there, and be sure to tuck your knees as you're in the air, you can't help but go over. It's a cinch! Watch me." And with that, he leapt high and flew through the air, his body becoming a tight ball of energy as it curled into itself and spun backwards not two, but three times. The others gasped. Nancy grimaced.

"Now you try it," he offered, a cocky smile on his broad face.

"No thanks. I couldn't begin to duplicate that." She was so curt with him, even Ardith looked up in surprise. Nancy was usually happy to get help from anyone who'd offer it.

"Enough of that for today. Let's work on the cheers. Josh has to know the most basic by Saturday. Mary Ellen, let's go over the 'Tiger,' 'Victory,' and 'Beat 'Em' cheers this afternoon. We don't want to overwhelm you, Josh, but there's a lot to learn."

"Hey, that's fine with me," Josh said with a shrug. "I'm having a ball. This is fun."

Angie distinctly heard Nancy mutter, "I'm glad *you* think so," and, while Mary Ellen was showing Josh where to stand, gave Nancy a sideways kick in the ankle.

"Straighten up, will you?" Angie hissed. "Whatever's bothering you about him will have to wait."

Nancy took her place, which happened to be between Walt and Josh, and stood facing the mirror as if it was her executioner.

"Now," Ardith instructed, "the cheer begins with you two guys holding Nancy under the arms. On the second line, we all start high kicks, and you lift her while she's kicking and help her to flip over backwards. Got it? Let's try it."

The six of them just couldn't get it together. Whether it was the mood of despair, the awkwardness of having a newcomer, or Nancy's ter-

65

rible attitude, the thing would not gel, no matter how many times they tried it. They went from one cheer to the next, and although Josh seemed to be picking up the steps easily, the overall effect was one of chaos. When the clock on the far wall hit six, Ardith stopped them with a sigh.

"All right, let's quit, shall we? Look, kids, we really don't have a lot of time. Tomorrow, I want to see you warmed up and ready to go by three-thirty, and then we'll work on the cheers themselves all afternoon. But you have to concentrate — *you* have to make it happen. If any of you have any thoughts about this not working, then it won't." She was looking directly at Nancy. "So leave your little concerns and big problems home tomorrow, will you?" She turned on her heel and swiftly left the room, and the kids breathed a sigh of relief. One by one, they started toward the showers. Josh looked at Nancy as she passed him at the door, but she didn't look back. She marched stolidly down the hall and followed Mary Ellen into the locker room.

"Now," Angie asked Nancy when the four girls were alone, stripping out of their clothes, "would you care to explain?"

Mary Ellen and Olivia were both staring at Nancy. There was no way she could avoid their annoyed and curious eyes.

"Josh Breitman is the son of my parents' best friends," she moaned.

"So?" Olivia was unyielding. "What does that have to do with anything?"

"Ever since we moved to Tarenton, they've been after me to date him. At family events, the

Breitmans always show up, and there's Josh. At summer barbecues, there's Josh. I mean, it should be clear to everyone by now that we're not interested in each other and never will be. But they keep pushing it!"

"Why?" Mary Ellen stuck a shower cap over her gleaming hair and threw a towel over her elegant white shoulder. "I mean, if it's not love at first sight — or second, or tenth — why bother?"

"Because, don't you see?" Nancy ran her hands through her thick, dark hair. "He's a nice Jewish boy. He's smart. He's probably going to get into Harvard. He's everything they ever wanted for me. Ugh!"

Angie couldn't help but laugh, although she felt for her friend. "But what's he like as a person?" she demanded.

"Oh, you know, conceited, stuck on himself."

"I didn't see that in him today." Olivia shrugged. "I suppose he could have been nervous and all, it being his first day, but —"

"Josh Breitman is never nervous. He's the cockiest kid I ever met," Nancy said decisively. "You saw that demonstration on the minitramp when I botched it. You don't call that nerve?"

"He was just trying to help," Angie offered. Then she shook her head and sat next to Nancy on the wooden bench. "Look, no matter how you felt about him in the past, you have to ditch it for now. What's important is getting us all to work like a team, and we'll never manage that if you're set on keeping up this feud, right?"

"Promise you'll try," Olivia begged her. "And who knows, you might get to like him after all."

Nancy wrinkled her face. "You've got to be kidding."

"Just *try*!" Mary Ellen insisted. "Pretend it's. . . ." She nearly said Ben Adamson and caught herself just in time. "Pretend it's your knight in shining armor."

"Pretend it's Pres," Angie said quietly. The others were suddenly silent, each of them realizing that, for all their complaining and being annoyed, they missed him. They knew he must be suffering, too. He'd just been given notice that he no longer belonged, and that had to be devastating to anyone's ego, let alone his. And just when he'd taken on all his own personal demons, he had to assume responsibility for splitting up the team, too.

"I'll try," Nancy agreed. "But it's not going to be easy." She thrust her face into her hands and shook her head in misery. "I've been so nice to people lately — I even helped some little kids cross a street last night. I don't deserve this! And the worst part is, my parents will find out and then they'll start a total campaign. 'Elect Josh Breitman Boyfriend of the Year.' Yuk!"

The other girls laughed, but tenderly. None of them could really make fun of Nancy's plight. Aside from the fact that they liked her a lot, every one of them knew that it could have been them. When it came to matters of the heart, nobody escaped.

As Mary Ellen showered and changed, she kept relating Nancy's problem to her own. She'd never stand for it if someone came along and designated the one boy for her. If her father put

68

his foot down and said, all right, it's Pres Tilford and that's it, or it's Donny Parrish and I don't want to hear any guff about it, she'd undoubtedly rebel and lose interest in both of them. In India, she remembered, they still had arranged marriages. Sometimes, the poor bride didn't even see the groom until their wedding day! It was positively weird!

She threw on her blackwatch-plaid skirt and high-necked white blouse, tucked up the few wheat-colored tendrils that had fallen out of place, and raced out of the locker room. Donny hated it when she kept him waiting, and his practice was generally over before hers. Naturally, he showered and was ready in no time.

She was halfway down the corridor when she felt a tug on her arm. Suddenly she was being whirled around, and she felt giddy even before she saw the tall shape clearly before her.

"Let me take you home tonight," Patrick breathed. He was wearing his white coveralls, the uniform he always wore when he was working. His wide mouth was smiling gently, and she could feel the heat behind his offer.

"I . . . someone's waiting for me. In the parking lot," she answered needlessly, her voice cracking. No, she couldn't walk out there with him! He'd probably even parked his garbage truck somewhere near Donny's Chevy — on purpose, to embarrass her!

"Let him wait. I know you want to." Patrick didn't need to say more. He pulled her close against him. His mouth hovered over hers, threatening and tantalizing, both at once. Nobody was around. Mary Ellen could hear only the distant sound of the floor waxer, as the janitor hummed away down the corridor, going in the opposite direction. No one would see them, and how she wanted to kiss those full, warm lips!

"Listen, Patrick, this is just impossible." She squirmed slightly in his grasp, but not enough to sever their delicious contact. "When are you going to get the message?"

"I've got the message. Sweetie, what you say and what you mean are two different things entirely. You know it as well as I do." And then he kissed her, deliberately and thoroughly, leaving no room for doubt as to how he felt and what he wanted. She clung to him hopelessly, realizing she was lost and hating herself for it.

She *did* care about Patrick, and that was the awful part. Her heart was his, and had been for a long time. It was just her stupid sense of propriety, of what she pictured for herself further along the road, that stopped her from giving in entirely. He was never going to change, never going to want more than his lucrative garbage route and a nice house in Tarenton and a comfortable suburban life. She couldn't settle for that! She just wouldn't!

"I've got to go," she muttered, wrenching away. Once she broke out of his embrace, she could breathe again, but it was still hard to think.

"Run if you want to." He shrugged, looking very pleased with himself. "I have all the time in the world, and believe me, babe, I've got longer legs. This race is an open and shut case." And then, to her amazement, *he* walked away from her, whistling a silly little tune as he swaggered toward the stairwell. *Guys*, honestly!

As she ran to the parking lot, she still tingled everywhere Pat had touched her. And when Donny blew the horn at her, she hardly heard it. She walked toward his car dreamily, the evening breeze taking her neat hairdo and adding its own finishing touches. Like her feelings, she thought as she let the wind carry the blonde strands wherever it would, she just couldn't stop them.

"Your lipstick's smeared," Donny said when he saw her.

"And I'm late, don't tell me." She gave him a peck on the cheek, self-consciously dabbing at the pink stain she left there. Patrick had most of it, of course, and he probably hadn't bothered to wipe it off. Was there something wrong with her that she could behave this way with two different boys within minutes of each other? Not that she'd done anything really reprehensible, but still. . . .

"There's that guy with the garbage again," Donny muttered, as he turned on his headlights and pulled out of the parking lot. "He sure gets around," he laughed. "Well, forget about that creep. How was your day?" He reached for her hand, and she let him take it, but there was very little enthusiasm in her response. She wanted Donny to be *it*, to be the one she not only was proud to be seen with, but also the one who made her stop in her tracks, made her breathless with excitement. Unfortunately, it wasn't like that with them. They dated, they had stuff to talk about, they were both pretty big socially at school, and that was all.

Mary Ellen sat beside him in silence on the way home. Would her choices be any easier if she weren't involved with any boys at all, if she only had herself to depend on for emotional support? No, things would be miserable without guys. But why did they have to make everything so messy? She was beginning to think that an arranged marriage might not be so stupid after all. At least it would take the confusion out of her life!

Pres left school early. There was nothing to be gained by hanging around, and Kerry had a drama society meeting till late, so he might as well split. If he went to the library and waited for her, he'd probably run into the guys from the team coming down from practice, and that was the last thing he wanted. Boy, what a lousy deal — to toss him out on his ear without a day's warning, without so much as an afternoon's detention! And they'd even gone behind his back and gotten a replacement already — some kid, some senior who measured about five-foot-zero, according to Vanessa, who'd wasted no time in telling him. What a bummer!

He got in the car and drove, covering the few miles of the town a couple of times before heading out toward Narrow Brook Lake. He found himself winding around back into town, and suddenly, he was terribly hungry. There was nothing that would taste as good right now as a burger and fries, washed down with a chocolate milkshake. The problem was where to go. If he stopped at Pete's, the whole crowd would be there. Too early for the team, but the whole rest of his class'd be there, practically. And they'd all be talking about him. How could he show his face there? With Kerry, he might have considered it. But alone, forget it.

Nowhere to go. Nothing to do. The idea of a warmed-up TV dinner at James's studio was more than he could take. He drove back to school and sat in the parking lot again, hoping something would happen. Anything.

"Isn't that Pres?" Olivia peered out of the Jeep's windshield in the gathering dark. "What's he doing back here?"

"Waiting for us, maybe?" Walt offered. He had his arm around her, and was feeling pretty mellow. His limbs were tired and all stretched out from the difficult practice, and had been burnished to a fine glow in the hot shower. And he was even warmer because of the presence of the small, delicate girl beside him.

"You want to go talk to him?" Olivia had her hand on the door handle, but Walt leaned over and snapped the lock.

"Not really. I'd rather kiss you."

She smiled into the dark, but shook her head slightly. "I want to talk first. What do you think of the new guy?"

"He's okay. I guess he could even work out." Walt shrugged. "But he'll never be part of the team." He was disappointed, longing for a kiss, but figured it could wait if it had to. Immediate gratification was nice, but not always practical.

"You mean he's a hog for his own glory, right?" she grinned. "A John McEnroe type?"

"Like some people are part of the chorus, but others just have to sing the solo." Walt laughed and thumped the steering wheel. "Listen to me! Making like Pres is some kind of self-sacrificing, lovable pushover."

"Like you?" Olivia teased, unsnapping the lock behind her.

"Exactly." Walt snapped the lock again. "Okay, we've talked. Come here, you beautiful, smart, wonderful girl."

"I want to see Pres," Olivia said decisively. "That doesn't mean I don't want to see you." She kissed him lightly, then thought better of it and kissed him again, this time lingeringly and happily. "I hate making out in cars," she grumbled as she dodged his hands and undid the lock, slipping out of the Jeep like a shadow. "Come on!"

Walt lumbered behind her, savoring his good fortune. She was a girl who said what she meant, at least. And she meant she wanted to be with him, which was the best part of all.

"Pres!" Olivia yelled. "Hey, it's us!"

Pres rolled down the window of the Porsche, half delighted and half embarrassed to have been spotted. "How's it goin'?" he asked casually, as if today had been a day like any other and he was just sitting there, waiting for the light to change.

"We missed you," Walt answered. "We want you back, man."

"Sure. Tell it to the judge."

"But you could move back with your folks and solve the whole thing," Olivia begged. "Believe me, I'm an expert when it comes to running-away-from-home schemes. I've got so many plots to escape my mother's clutches, I could write a Gothic novel. But I don't act on them because there are things I want more — like cheering. Can we come inside? It's getting cold."

"Be my guest," Pres shrugged, opening the door on the passenger side, and watched his two ex-teammates climb in. And then he noticed that Walt had his arm around Olivia and he felt even more miserable than he had a few minutes ago.

"What's the deal?" Walt asked him. "Just tell us why."

"I want to be free, man," Pres said in a muffled tone. "That's the bottom line. I'm sorry to mess you guys up, but you've got somebody else, right? Hey, I was just another gorgeous body. You'll get over me."

"Not true." Olivia's stern, heart-shaped face was shaded with a variety of emotions. "You were one of us."

Pres's flippant words died in his throat. He sat there, his hands gripping the steering wheel, until finally Walt and Olivia got out of the car and walked away.

CHAPTER

The Tarenton games were always well attended, but this one was packed. There were no seats at all left in the gym bleachers, and the fans who were determined to get in had jammed themselves along the rear doors of the gym.

"It would have to be a full house our first time out," Angie mumbled, adjusting the pleats of her cheering skirt. There had been a last-minute panic about Josh's uniform, because, of course, he was too short to fit into Pres's. But Rose Poletti came to the rescue when her daughter begged her, quickly altering an extra pair of scarlet pants with the white stripe down the seams as well as the white sweater with the scarlet "T" for Josh. He looked great, Angie thought.

Nancy was jumping rope in the corner of the practice room, her white pleats unfolding and overlapping against the scarlet skirt every time she went up and down. It had been a grueling week, and her spirits were no better than they

76

had been on Tuesday, when this whole thing started.

On Wednesday, during practice, Josh had held her in the air just a minute too long and later, had hung around so that he could meet her at her car. On Thursday, he'd stuffed a silly panda bear in her locker with a note attached that read, "I'm really not so hard to bear." On Friday, he'd come up to her at lunchtime and demanded to be allowed to sit with her. What could she do? She just couldn't figure out why he was going to such lengths to spend time with a girl he'd purposely shunned for the past year and a half.

Olivia and Walt sat together at Nancy's feet, doing two-person stretches. They looked kind of funny holding hands with their feet spread wide, rocking back and forth like one big seesaw, Olivia's short legs coming only to Walt's muscular calves, but they seemed to be having a wonderful time. Mary Ellen glanced over at them from her backbend and considered them. They were going home together every night now, and they seemed to appear and disappear at exactly the same moment. Was it possible? Little Olivia and big clown Walt?

"Well, what are you all standing around for?" Ardith bustled into the room like a whirlwind, her hair tousled, as though she'd been running her fingers through it for the past hour. "It's late, kids. I know you can do it. Just concentrate on your moves and remember what game you're cheering for. Whatever you do, don't yell for any touchdowns."

She laughed at her feeble attempt at a joke.

Tarenton was the only school in the district whose football and basketball seasons overlapped. This caused occasional upsets among the players who were on both teams, and perennial confusion among the fans. "Josh, how are you feeling? You think you can do it?" Ardith ran her sentences together to save time.

"Great. Never been better." Stealthily, he maneuvered himself over to Nancy and jumped into her next turn of the rope. She stopped moving abruptly and they bumped heads.

"I'll line us up, then," Mary Ellen suggested. She patted her golden hair and, catching a glimpse of her perfect profile in the glass panel of the door, she decided she was ready. With determined steps, she led the way toward the rear gym door. The others, bouncing on their toes, were right behind her.

"And one, and two. . . ." She began the cheer before opening the door. This was one the whole crowd knew, so it didn't matter if they heard every word clearly.

> "We're here for you!
> And three and four,
> Let's mop up the floor!
> And five and six,
> Just watch our tricks!
> Seven, eight, nine,
> Stayin' right on line!
> Tarenton — you're a ten!
> Yay!"

Mary Ellen kept a close eye on Josh as he

cartwheeled his way to the center of the floor and the others flipped or somersaulted around him, but she really didn't have to. The guy knew what he was doing. He was working into the routine as though he had done it a thousand times, and had even made it his own. Pres, the great cartwheeler of all times, had a smooth, even pattern to his turns, but Josh seemed to bounce all the time. It was kind of cute.

As Mary Ellen looked up from her place, a wide smile on her lovely face, the cheer springing from her throat fully and happily, she knew the crowd loved her. It was times like this that fulfilled her and made her dissatisfied all at once. Cheering gave her a tantalizing taste of what it might be like when she was a model, coming down that runway to the applause of every top designer in New York. It made her feel as if she was riding a swing, being pushed higher and faster. It was like delirium, like a fever.

She came out of a fast spin into Walt's waiting arms and held a second, her eyes taking in the second row of the bleachers. For an instant, the smile faded from her face. There were Pres and Kerry, holding hands, looking on in grim anticipation. She knew that scowl of his all too well. It must be eating him alive to be here and not be with them, to have to sit on the sidelines.

She spun again and now she was facing Patrick, who was grinning directly at her with a really ridiculous expression on his face. He did look terrific today. When he stood up to cheer the cheerleaders, she couldn't help but notice his sharp Fair Isle vest over the starched white

79

shirt and those neat gray cords. The guy really had it all together, she sighed to herself as she took a turn away from Walt and Angie and led the way, clapping and yelling, toward the door where the Tarenton basketball team was straining to burst through.

"Tarenton,
In the sun!
Tarenton,
You're the one!
Son of a gun!
Ready to run!
Beat 'em! Beat 'em! Yay!"

The "Beat 'Em" cheer was nearly drowned out by the sound of the crowd, welcoming each player to the floor. As Donny passed Mary Ellen, he grabbed her hand for a second, but let go so quickly that no one noticed. The rest of his team followed him, ready for a victory, tasting the win they knew was nearly theirs.

The Muskeagtown Maulers ran out next, their own cheering team trying to outdo Tarenton's — in volume if nothing else. They had some good players, but the Tarenton Wolves were generally considered to be the best team in the district, running neck and neck with Garrison High. With Donny Parrish, their power forward, and Hank Vreewright, the star center, they couldn't miss tonight.

The two teams lined up as the cheerleaders took their places on the sidelines, stepping over the fans who crowded the aisles. The referee threw the ball up between the two centers and Hank tapped it first. The game was on.

The first half was wild, the score hovering at a tie the entire time. One of the Muskeagtown shooters was really hot tonight, which put Donny on his toes. Nearly every time he captured the ball and dribbled it down the floor, he eluded the defense and lined himself up for the best shot. If he couldn't shoot, he'd pass, but you could tell it was costing him something to give the ball away.

"These guys are terrific," Josh whispered to Nancy as they stood working the crowd, giving the "Growl, Wolves, Growl!" cheer.

"Haven't you ever seen a basketball game before?" she asked sarcastically.

"Not with you. My eyes have been opened to all sorts of new things," he grinned. Nancy looked at the ceiling and took Mary Ellen's cue for the "Victory" cheer.

But at that moment, something seemed to distract Donny, just as he was about to shoot. The six-foot-seven Muskeagtown center easily knocked the ball from his hand and passed it downcourt to one of his open teammates. The Muskeagtown guard made a long shot, a three-pointer, and that wrapped up the first half of the game. The visiting team's cheerleaders went wild. They were winning.

Mary Ellen started the halftime routines with less than the gung-ho spirit the squad needed. Josh was the only one who was still bouncing, and even Angie's straddle jumps lacked oomph. They were all super-aware of Pres, now sitting glumly, now getting up to shake a fist, or make a face, or both. It was like having Big Brother watching.

"C'mon, Donny," Mary Ellen whispered, as they retreated for the second half of the game. "Show 'em what's what."

But Donny wasn't concentrating. It was evident from the beginning, when he simply stopped guarding his Muskeagtown opposite and started watching something — or someone — in the bleachers.

"What is he *doing*?" Olivia asked in a panic, even though it was strictly forbidden to talk at games. Nothing was supposed to distract them from what was happening on the court. "Donny never lets anything get in the way of a win."

Mary Ellen had known all along; actually, she'd seen the problem coming before Donny did. Every time she moved, every cheer she led, Patrick got up and started blowing kisses at her.

"Donny, don't look at him," she pleaded under her breath. It was too late, though. As the clock ran down to almost nothing, he fouled, and then, unbelievably, fouled again. When the ball finally was back in play, he let Muskeagtown make three baskets in a row. His teammates were looking at him as though they wanted to kill. Ahead 64-59, Muskeagtown simply ran out the clock, practically rubbing Tarenton's nose in it, to win the game.

The Muskeagtown cheerleaders filed onto the court in triumph several seconds later, doing a splashy windup routine that had at least half the crowd on their feet. The Tarenton kids and their parents looked angry and disappointed as they made their way out of the gym, and the cheerleaders could scarcely wait to disappear. Mary Ellen didn't want to see Donny, didn't want to get anywhere near him. It was so embarrassing — she knew the whole awful thing was her fault.

She passed Vanessa, just climbing down from the bleachers, and looked the other way. But Donny was coming right toward her, and suddently she felt trapped — nowhere to run.

"Well, that was *quite* a performance, Mr. Parrish," Vanessa cooed at Donny, who was dripping with sweat, his shoulders hunched under the thin towel his coach had thrown at him. "Congratulations! You just about lost that game single-handedly." She positively oozed venom.

"Shut up, Vanessa," Mary Ellen said, for some reason jumping to Donny's defense.

"Now why do you think we lost, Melon?" Vanessa sounded really interested. "Do you have any idea?" With that, she walked away, head held high. Mary Ellen would have liked nothing better than to wipe that smirk off her face, but Donny stopped her.

"Look," he said softly. "I know I didn't do my best, and I feel rotten about it, but how could I concentrate with what was going on out there? This has to stop. Did you see that guy, making a fool of himself over you? It was disgusting."

"Donny, get dressed. We'll talk about this some other time." She wanted to be furious with him for losing, but some part of her felt oddly flattered. She meant more to him than the game! His feelings for her were that strong!

"No, I want to talk about it *now*. That bozo thinks he owns you, and you've got to set him straight."

"That's not true. Patrick and I —"

"Used to have something going."

"That's a lie!" she fumed. "We never did. I never let him hope that —"

"Hey, he wouldn't behave that way if you didn't!" Donny was yelling now, but they were alone in the gym, so it didn't matter. Donny's usually placid features were distorted with rage, and he had that fierce, powerful look he sometimes got when an opponent on the court handed him a real challenge. "Mary Ellen, I can't take this being played off against another guy. You better make up your mind. One or the other — not both of us. That's all I have to say." He stalked away from her, his long legs striding swiftly to the gym door and out into the corridor.

Slowly, Mary Ellen sank down on the nearest bleacher and put her head in her hands. He was right, of course. If she wasn't leading Patrick on, she certainly wasn't turning him off. And it was Donny she wanted to be with. Wasn't it? Of course, it had to be. He was captain of the basketball team, tall, handsome, lived in a lovely home near the lake, really popular at school. At least, she thought ruefully as she got up and made her way to the locker room, he was popular until tonight. After what he'd done, there probably wasn't a kid in school who still thought of him as a hero. What she still couldn't figure out was whether he ever had been.

* * *

Josh was dressed before Walt, so, after saying good-night to his new teammate, he slung his sheepskin jacket over his shoulder and walked down to the girls' locker room. He slid down the wall and sat cross-legged, barring the way. She's be out in a minute or so.

He felt pretty good about the game, actually. Of course he wasn't thrilled that Tarenton had lost, and probably nobody would remember his performance because of that, but at least he'd shown the squad that he could do it. Not that he'd ever doubted it, really, but it was vital to have other people know his worth. If there was one thing his dad drummed into him over the years, it was the importance of getting along, and of making a good impression. He carried that a little too far sometimes, but in this case, it was working.

But was it working with Nancy? He knew she was pretty mixed up about him, and that was only natural. After all, they'd avoided each other like the bubonic plague for a year and a half. He'd always thought she was a real bubble-brain, just another dumb girl, but when he'd seen her Tuesday, working out with the squad, he'd seen an entirely different person. He admired people who committed themselves to something, who worked hard to get what they wanted. Not to mention the fact that she was a damn sexy, good-looking girl.

The door opened and Olivia walked out, followed by Angie. They both looked devastated, and his infectious grin did nothing to revive their spirits.

"Hey, you win some, you lose some," he said with false cheer, standing up to greet them.

"Josh, we shouldn't have lost this one," Olivia pointed out.

"By the way, Josh," Angie said, smiling kindly. "You were awfully good. I don't know how you did it, but you have all the routines down without a hitch. You're doing a brilliant job."

"Really," Olivia chimed in.

He was just about to thank them for the compliment when Nancy walked out the locker room door. He thought she looked fantastic, her complexion ruddy from the shower, her dark eyes vibrant and oh, so deep. When she saw him, she hesitated a second, then her hand flew nervously to her hair.

"How about a Coke?" he asked her in front of the other two. He really would have preferred waiting until they were alone, but he was worried she might run off if he didn't pounce immediately.

"I don't think so. Not tonight. My parents are waiting out in the parking lot."

"They wouldn't mind," he grinned knowingly.

They'd be tickled pink, Nancy thought. The kid was maddening. He still annoyed her, but there was something kind of appealing about him, if you liked that type.

"Well, Walt is probably wondering where I am," Olivia cut in, taking Angie by the arm.

"And I'm going out with some of the guys," Angie said mysteriously. Since her breakup with Marc, she'd dated sporadically, but everyone seemed to know she was still tender from her wounds, so there was nothing serious going on.

"See you Monday. 'Bye!" Josh waved at them deliriously as they beat a hasty retreat down the corridor. He faced Nancy, his hands on his hips. "Well?"

"Josh, I really don't —"

"You don't hate me, do you?" he asked frankly, softly.

"Of course not." She smiled indulgently.

"I'm not really that terrible. If our parents hadn't introduced us, you'd probably jump at the opportunity."

That did it. Why, of all the conceited, arrogant. . . ! "Josh, why don't you go cool off your swelled head in the night air. It'll do you good." She stormed past him, her boot heels clicking on the marble floors.

"Wait! Hey, give me a chance, would you, Nancy?" He was pleading now, all his self-assurance slowly waning away. "I didn't mean anything by that. I just think we're at an unfair disadvantage. You know, when your parents tell you to do something, you naturally run in the opposite direction. So, taking that into consideration, I would like — really I would — to start all over again, as if we didn't know each other. Hello, I'm Josh Breitman."

She stared at him for a second, then gave a funny, exasperated laugh. "Why are you trying so hard?" she asked quietly.

"Because I get a kick out of all this *trouble* you're giving me, is why," he joked.

She shut her eyes tight, wondering why she was so compelled to go out with him at the very

87

same time that she wanted him to leave her alone. "Well, maybe just a Coke," she sighed.

"Super! Great! Well. . . ." He made a wide flourish toward the stairs. "Shall we?"

"Just let me . . . I have to go tell my folks. I'll meet you by your car," she explained, suddenly anxious all over again.

"If you don't want to say it's me you're going out with, you don't have to." Josh smiled lightly. "If that would make it easier for now."

She looked at him curiously, amazed that he knew her worst fears and that he was so easy about letting her off the hook. He *knew* her parents would jump all over her with how thrilled they were that she'd finally seen the light about their friends' son, and he *knew* that would be awful for her. Suddenly, she liked him. He understood her. Was that partly, she wondered, because they came from the same kind of background?

"I'll see you at your car in ten," she promised, already speeding down the stairs.

Josh stood in the empty corridor, threw his sheepskin coat in the air, and gave the "Victory" cheer to the still air.

"Pres, let's go. It's stupid to hang around here," Kerry said, pulling on his arm. The parking lot was deserted, but Pres hadn't moved from his position behind the old maple tree since the game started letting out forty minutes ago.

Pres didn't move. He had rarely felt lower, even when he was fighting with his father.

"Look, they lost the game. But they would

88

have anyway, you cheering or not. It has nothing to do with you," Kerry said.

"Of course it does!" he exploded at her. When she jumped back, he took her by both shoulders and pulled her to him. "Sorry, I shouldn't take it out on you. Kerry, it's not only losing, don't you see? It's that shrimpy kid doing my stuff. It's the rest of the squad. They'll probably never speak to me again. Just like my folks," he added with a sardonic grin.

"Why don't you call your mom?" Kerry asked quietly. "You could say hi and then hang up." When he was silent, she added, "It wouldn't kill you."

He put his arm around her and started to walk her toward the car. "Maybe I should call the kids. Talk to them . . . I don't know."

"Maybe you shouldn't worry so much." Kerry leaned up and stood on her toes to plant a kiss on his lips. He responded immediately, crushing her to him as he pressed his mouth over hers. They stayed like that for a long time, held together by a feeling that rocked them both. When at last Kerry pulled away, Pres was staring down at her, a trembling smile covering up for his childish fears. He needed her — he really did — and it took a lot out of him to admit that.

"Don't go anywhere, will you, Kerry?" he asked softly when they started back to the car. "Stick by me."

"Like glue," she promised solemnly, and she meant it.

CHAPTER

It was a beautiful Sunday morning. Even the birds had forgotten how cold it was and were ducking merrily in and out of tree branches, doing all the silly aeronautical maneuvers birds do when the weather suits them. Pres had rolled up the sleeves of his flannel shirt and was splitting logs for the wood stove. Uncle James was parked on a nearby tree stump, drinking pitch-black coffee, and contentedly watching his nephew work.

"You have a real aptitude for that, you know?" he commented. "Look at those splits now, just as clean as lightning. I think you should go into the lumbering business."

"Oh yeah?" Pres lifted an eyebrow at him. "You're only saying that to get me to cut extra for you."

"Not true. I know an artist when I see one, and you're one."

"Hey, if you call this art, you better hang up your easel," Pres teased. He stopped a moment, spit on his chilled hands and rubbed them, then grabbed the ax handle again.

"Well, how do you like living alone?" his uncle asked, more serious now. "Is it all you thought it was cracked up to be?"

"Sure," Pres lied. "It's great. Do what I want when I want, come and go without anyone looking over my shoulder. It's the life, man."

"And I was thinking you were looking kinda peaked lately," James said, getting up and starting toward the main house. "Shows how observant I am." He could tell that Pres just wasn't ready to tell him the truth. "Want some fresh-brewed coffee?" he offered.

"It that what you call that stuff?" Pres glanced quizzically at James's stained cup. "I thought it was diesel fuel."

Laughing, James started back to the house, but he stopped and turned at the sound of a car coming up the road. Pres saw it at the same time and cursed, then planted the ax firmly in the wood before him.

"I'll bring two cups," James said. "Looks like you're going to need it strong," he grimaced, and quickly vanished into the house. This was no time to stick around.

Mrs. Preston Tilford II parked the black Mercedes beside the studio and slowly, she got out of the car.

Pres stared at his mother as though she were someone else. He'd seen that gray skirt hundreds of times, and that camel's hair jacket with its matching beret. He'd seen her fine-boned, aristo-cratic face a lot lately, when he was lying in front of the fire just about to fall asleep, and he'd known every expression on it for eighteen years now. And yet, she didn't *seem* like his mother. She was different somehow.

"Hello, Pres," she said, standing about five feet away. The breeze tugged at her hat, and she pulled it down firmly over her dark, graying hair.

"Hi." What was he going to say? What should he do? "You . . . ah, want to come in?" he asked politely.

"Thank you. That would be fine," she nodded.

They were being so careful with each other! He couldn't stand it. And where was James with the coffee? He shouldn't be expected to go through this by himself.

Together, they walked into the small studio, where the fire was crackling.

"Have a seat," he offered graciously.

She sat, neatly arranging her skirt around her. He sat opposite on the unmade bed, then jumped up when he noticed the carton of milk sitting on the counter. She always hated it when he left the milk out to sour at home.

"Pres. . . ."

"Mom. . . ." They began at the same time, and both laughed nervously. "Ah, you first."

"Listen, Pres. I would have called this week, but your father convinced me that I should wait. And then I decided to come on over, just in case."

"In case of what?"

"Well, it did occur to us that you might hang up if we called." She wasn't the least bit nervous

92

about saying this, he noticed. She assumed he hated them!

"I wouldn't have," he told her quickly. "Anyhow, it's good you came. This way you get to see I'm in a nice place, doing great on my own, right?"

"Dear," she said, sitting forward in her seat, "I want you back. Very badly." Her face didn't betray much. She hardly ever cried, although Pres liked to think that maybe she'd shed a few tears over him in the past few days. Now, however, she was totally dry-eyed.

"*You* want me back — what about him?"

"Well, your father, naturally . . . he does, too."

"So why didn't he come with you?" Pres demanded, covering the small room in three strides. "If he cares so much, why didn't *he* ask me to come home?"

"He's got his pride." She shrugged. "He doesn't like to beg. And he didn't want to put himself in the position of losing his temper with you. That never solves anything."

"He's mad, huh?" Pres asked.

"What do you expect? Pres, he was trying to do something helpful for you. He never dreamed you'd take offense, let alone run off like you did. For heaven's sake, he got you a job! He didn't like to see you wasting your time with —"

Pres cut her off quickly. "With stuff like cheerleading. With normal stuff like hanging out with my friends."

His mother gave him a disparaging look. "Oh, dear, you really don't understand him at all."

"Yeah, well, he doesn't get me either. So it's

just as well we're not living together anymore."

Felicia Tilford shook her head, then stood up, wondering whether it would do any good at all to try another tactic. "I've been talking to Mrs. Oetjen," she told him. "And I know you're on probation. You're off the squad anyway, Pres, so what does it gain you to persist in this . . . this silly game?"

"Mom," he said between clenched teeth, "if you think it's a game, you have a lot to learn about me. This is a decision I made, for good or bad. I'm happy here, which is more than I could ever say about being home."

She turned away suddenly, but he caught a glimpse of tears glistening in her eyes. He'd hurt her, and he was glad of it.

"I'm sorry to hear you say this, but I don't think you really mean it, so I won't argue." She marched briskly to the door, stopping with her hand on the knob. "You can always come back — I want you to know that," she said in a much softer tone. And then, to his amazement, she walked over and roughly kissed him on the cheek. He couldn't remember the last time she'd kissed him.

After she left, he stood by the door, listening to the sound of the car's engine starting up and moving away. He wanted to forget the whole incident, but hard as he tried, it stayed with him. *She* stayed with him, and he hated her for it.

It was about four when he heard the sound of another car on the road, and then a second coming right after it. He peered out the window into the afternoon sun.

Could that be Walt's Jeep? And it looked like Nancy's mother's car following it. He grinned, then leapt out the door like a crazy person, waving his arms and dancing around the yard.

Walt blared the Jeep's horn and pulled alongside the studio, spraying gravel. Olivia had jumped down before the car had come to a complete stop and she waved back at Pres, mimicking his ridiculous dance in the middle of the road.

"So, how's everything?" Angie called, stepping out of Nancy's car. Mary Ellen joined her, shading her eyes to get a better look at James's house. Nancy and Walt brought up the rear, their arms full of packages and bags.

"Everything's *great*." Pres nodded, still grinning. "C'mon in and see my place. What's all this?" he asked, gesturing at the paraphernalia they'd brought.

"Well, everyone knows a young bachelor has no idea how to keep house for himself." Angie laughed, as Pres opened the door for them and ushered them inside. "So we've come to help you make this house a home. Well, will you look at that!" She stared, wide-eyed, at the painting in progress on the easel. It was pretty abstract, but no one could miss the subject matter. A green-limbed man with pink toes was passionately embracing a blue and yellow woman with a very large belly.

"My uncle's latest," Pres said apologetically.

"Must be kind of weird having that facing you when you get up in the morning, huh?" Walt wandered around the small space, taking in the roughhewn wooden beams and smooth soapstone

95

mantel over the wood stove. "Other than that, it's cool. I like it," he pronounced decisively. "What do you guys think?"

"Terrific," Mary Ellen sighed. She could just imagine herself here in a little hideaway when she'd tired of the nightlife of the big city and needed an escape. She and some devastatingly handsome movie producer would come up here, light a fire, and never answer the telephone.

"It's a little stark," Nancy said, running her hand along the kitchen counter. "How about some curtains, Pres? I made one once."

"You made *one* curtain?" Mary Ellen asked skeptically, sitting on the floor in front of the fire next to Olivia. "What happened to the other?"

"It died a horrible death in my mother's sewing machine. Don't ask me to describe it," Nancy shuddered in mock horror.

Angie gave her a playful push on the shoulder as she went to one of the shopping bags and withdrew a jar of popcorn kernels. "I don't know about anyone else, but I'm starved. Can we do this over the fire?"

"Why not?" Pres agreed, going to the refrigerator to get a six-pack of soda for everyone. He felt like a genial host, about a thousand percent better than he had twenty minutes ago. His pals had come to see him! They didn't hate him! With everyone pitching in to pour soda or heat the oil for the popcorn, it was like old times before he'd split the squad apart. And suddenly, he felt less guilty about it, like he could even talk about it.

"Kerry and I caught the game yesterday," he said casually, wandering over to the counter to turn on the small portable radio to a good rock station. "Pretty foul, if you ask me."

"Yeah, look who's talking," Walt said, grabbing an uncooked kernel from the pan and throwing it at Pres.

"Well, it was bad, man. That doofus Ardith got to replace me looked like he was trying out for the Olympic klutz award."

Everyone looked at Nancy, who turned three consecutive shades of crimson. "Oh, I don't think he's that awful," she said noncommittally. "After all, it was his first time out, and he'd only had four days to learn about a dozen routines. He'll get better."

"If you let him." Angie turned to Pres, then got up and moved closer to him. "It's all in your hands, you know."

"Don't start with me, Ange," Pres warned her. "I got a lecture from my mother this morning — I don't need five other parents."

"Hey, have you lost it completely?" Walt demanded. "You saddled us with a klutz from the word go *and* the hassle of teaching the kid everything from scratch. You know, that's a lot for the rest of us to handle."

"He's not a klutz," Mary Ellen said, looking at Nancy. "As a matter of fact, I think he's really good. He's got a special flair. Don't you think so, Olivia?"

They all caught her drift at once: Shame Pres into coming back. "I think he's dynamite," Olivia agreed. "Gives a breath of fresh air to the squad."

"Hey, you're stuck with him now." Pres shrugged, trying not to let them get to him. "You better like him."

The room was stilled by an awkward pause, the kind everybody wants to break but no one knows how to. Finally, Angie grabbed the pan off the fire and made a big deal of offering the popcorn around.

"Don't you have any clean bowls in here?" she asked, rummaging through his cupboards. "Honestly."

"What are we cooking tonight, anyhow?" Mary Ellen asked the others, ignoring Pres. "I think pot roast — how about it?" She fished in one of the bags and brought out a large slab of pinkish-red meat.

"What are you going to do with that?" Pres asked, wrinkling up his nose.

"Cook it, stupid." Angie put her hands on her hips in exasperation. "Don't tell me you never saw a pot roast before."

"Not before it was dead," Pres grimaced.

"Boy, this guy has a lot to learn." Nancy took the meat from Mary Ellen and went to the stove with it, where she began rummaging around for a pan.

"You're not going to start cooking that without sandblasting the stove, are you?" Mary Ellen asked in disgust as Nancy lit the gas. She reached up to run her finger over the stove top. "Ugh, how can you live like this, Pres? It's criminal."

"You take care of the stove, Melon, and you start seasoning the meat, Nancy. I'll do something about the bathroom, okay?" Olivia told

98

them, her mouth full of popcorn. "Did you bring the cleanser?"

"In the bag," Mary Ellen nodded, already busy with a sponge.

"And I'll do the laundry," Walt grinned. "I'm wonderful at laundry," he confided to Pres. "Where do you hide the stuff? No, wait," he said, a finger to the side of his nose. "I just got a whiff. I can find it myself."

"Don't forget to sort the colors," Mary Ellen yelled in to him.

Pres watched in amazement as the five cheerleaders whipped around the studio, dusting, polishing, and scrubbing. They were so enthusiastic about their tasks that he actually got interested. Like Tom Sawyer's fence before it was whitewashed, the dirty studio became a challenge too good to pass up. Pres Tilford, who had never done a lick of housework in his life, whose mother would have fallen over in a dead faint at the sight of him with a bucket and mop, started washing the floor.

At one point, Angie stopped peeling potatoes and looked at him curiously. "Oh, what I wouldn't give for a camera. A perfect blackmail shot," she giggled.

"What do you mean?" Pres growled.

"Big bad Pres with his hot car and his own digs and his sexy ladies — cleaning! No one would believe it!" Walt chuckled.

And then they all started laughing at him. He laughed, too, pelting them with popcorn, trying to stuff it down the girls' shirt fronts, getting it right back again in direct hits to the face and neck. They were so busy fighting, they didn't hear the door open, and for a minute didn't even see Uncle James standing there in amazement, staring at all of them.

"What in the name of. . . ?" he boomed.

The battle ended as quickly as it had begun.

"We're making this house into a home," Pres explained. "James, these are the guys on the squad. Guys, my uncle, who has so kindly provided me with a place to live."

Everyone murmured hellos and started cleaning up the popcorn.

"Well, I thought I smelled something funny." James shook his head, going over to the stove and peering inside.

"Stay for dinner, James? There's plenty," Pres offered.

"Hey, no thanks. Home cooking is a little more domesticity than I can possibly stand," James laughed. He was still looking around, noting the shining counters and dusted surfaces. "I thought kids were supposed to raise hell and mess things up."

"Right, Mr. Tilford," Mary Ellen said with her most appealing cheerleader smile. "But we do that *all* the time. It gets boring."

James gave her a lopsided grin and swiped some popcorn from the overflowing bowl before starting back toward the front door. Pres followed him. "How's your mom?" he asked Pres under his breath so the others couldn't hear.

Pres shrugged. "Old story: She wants me back, my dad doesn't. I'm staying right where I am — if it's okay with you," he added.

"I don't mind, kid, not in the slightest. But watch it with the cleaning. I don't want you to turn into a wimp under my roof, understand." With an unbelieving shake of his head, James left the six of them to their craziness.

"When do we eat?" Pres demanded, coming back to the group, relishing the wonderful smells and the comfort of being surrounded by friends — such extraordinary friends who would even forgive a louse like him.

"When you set the table, wise guy." Walt slapped some paper napkins into his hand.

Pres did as he was told, realizing as he did so that family wasn't always the people you were related to. Sometimes, he thought as he put a fork at each place, family was closer than blood.

CHAPTER

8

"Okay, kids, that's it for tonight," Ardith sighed, stretching from one side to the other. "Everything's looking basically all right except for the new tumbling cheer. Work on it, would you. I don't want *you* working harder, though, Olivia. One jump higher and you'll go through the roof."

Everyone except the leaping gazelle in question looked gratefully at Ardith. They did worry about Olivia every once in a while. She had an almost obsessive need to do better — regardless of how perfect her routines looked — and she was always trying for something more difficult, more daring. It was very nerve-racking for the rest of them, when they watched her propel herself into the air like a person shot out of a cannon. They were certain she was about to land on her spinal column and end it all.

"And Walt," Ardith continued, "try not to

land on top of everyone when you take that spread eagle. Looking good, Josh," she added quietly to the newest member of the team.

"Thanks," he nodded, following Nancy out the door of the gym. He was feeling okay about himself these days. After all, Tarenton had won the last three games they'd cheered for, and everyone now freely acknowledged that the cheerleaders were back in shape again. Naturally, a bunch of kids doing their splits and backbends didn't make the touchdowns or baskets, but the morale-building factor they provided was important — everybody said so.

The girls were almost at their locker room, and Josh hurried to catch up. "Hey, wait a sec," he called to Nancy, who didn't turn around.

"I think someone wants you," Angie whispered to her.

Nancy gave her a look. "You don't have to remind me," she muttered as Angie swept inside the locker room with Mary Ellen and Olivia giggling meaningfully behind her. "Yes?" she asked, turning to Josh.

"I was just wondering about the dance a week from Saturday."

"Yes?" Nancy repeated. She liked him, she actually enjoyed being with him, but he was so persistent! Every day after practice, he'd been waiting to take her home. And after she'd finally agreed to their first date, he simply assumed they were a couple, and was there every time she turned around. She tried being frosty, being flip, being almost rude. Then she demanded her privacy, saying that it was every American citizen's right. But he wore her down with flowers, with sticks of gum, with double-chocolate malteds. She hated to admit it, but he was growing on her, sort of like a vine you have to cut off a building after a number of years.

"Well, you do dance, don't you?" Josh asked, his black eyes devouring her.

"I could dance circles around you," Nancy proclaimed.

"Sure you could. I guess we'll have to see. I'll pick you up at eight," he nodded cockily, starting down the hall toward the guys' lockers.

"Just a second," she fumed. "I haven't said anything about going with you."

"But you are. You have to!" He rushed back, looking terribly upset. "It's destiny. Kismet. You and I were matched in heaven. That means we're stuck, boogying together till the earth turns cold."

"Josh, honestly!" She threw her hands up, and he grabbed them.

He kissed her lightly, but underneath the playfulness was a deeper feeling that Nancy responded to.

"Say it — tell me you love me. Tell me you *like* me for now. I'll settle." He looked so earnest and anxious, she had to laugh.

"I do. I like you despite my best intentions."

"Then the dance is on?"

"I guess." She shrugged, wresting her hands away and walking through the door of the girls' room. There was something she couldn't put her finger on, something new about him that made her feel silly and giddy. It wasn't like with other guys she'd gone out with. With Ben, for instance, everything had been intense and passionate. Every moment seemed to weigh heavily; every word had meaning. She had never wanted to keep her hands off Ben. Or wanted his off of her.

With Josh, it was easy, almost carefree. And it was weird, since she'd fought her parents so long and so hard on this very subject. For over a year, she'd protested that Josh was too short for her, too overbearing, too aggressive.

When the Goldsteins had first moved to Tarenton, her father had begged Nancy to join the temple youth group, and consequently, she had stayed as far away from the temple as possible. It wasn't that she was ashamed of being Jewish — the tradition meant a lot to her. It was just that she wanted another, more exciting destiny than her mother's. And when she'd first met Josh, he reminded her of everything she was familiar with.

Now, though, she saw something more in him. Oh, he still tried too hard to please, and he was still kind of stuck on himself, but he was stuck on her, too, and the attention was pretty nice. She couldn't tell her parents, though. They didn't know she was going out with him, and if *she* had anything to do with it, they weren't ever going to find out.

"You look gooney," Olivia said, sticking her head out of the shower and glancing at Nancy, who was waiting with a towel wrapped around her middle. The girls' volleyball team had just finished practice, and showers were at a premium.

"You're no one to talk," Nancy huffed at her,

sighing as one of the Eismar twins beat her to the next available stall. "I've never seen you dancing around like an idiot before, but now you do it every time Walt trips over you."

"Just to get out of his way." Olivia smiled coyly.

"Oh, admit it, Livvy." Angie came up behind them, her long hair twisted under the shower cap. "We know you two are an item."

"I think it's wonderful," Mary Ellen chimed in. She was already in her underwear, putting cream on her long, slender legs. "The two of you go so perfectly together. Like cars and gasoline."

"Like rock 'n' roll," Nancy agreed.

"Like ice cream and hot fudge sauce." Angie sighed, her mind never off its favorite subject for long.

Olivia grinned sheepishly at them. "All right, I confess. He's just about the ideal boyfriend. He even tolerates my mother. The other night when he took me home she kept flashing the porch lights at the Jeep. And when I didn't pay any attention, she marched right over and demanded I come in the house. I was out of my mind, naturally, but Walt just smiled at her and said good evening. He's amazing. Never loses his temper, even though I lose mine all the time."

Mary Ellen wandered away from the group, the smile still fixed on her face. She was pleased for Olivia, although she'd never been one to revel in another person's happiness. What was theirs was theirs, and it didn't touch her too much. It was difficult for her to be as enthusiastic as the others, given her present situation. There

106

was Donny, and then there was Patrick. It was a royal pain.

She glanced over at Angie as she drew up her navy blue tights, making sure that every wrinkle was pulled out and that the mended run didn't show. Now why should Angie be so thrilled for Olivia? — she didn't have anyone at all. Since Marc had ditched her, she'd made a point of playing the field, but Mary Ellen knew she didn't have a date for the dance. I could give her one of mine, she thought glumly, zipping her corduroy jumpsuit to the top with a neat flourish. But which one?

"Good-night, gang. Get some rest. That practice tomorrow is going to be a killer, I can tell." She stuffed her wet clothes into the old gym bag she carried, picked up her books, and started out of the locker room.

"See you tomorrow," Nancy sang, her thoughts on Josh.

"Have a good one," Olivia called out, rubbing herself thoroughly with her towel. Walt was probably doing the same thing right now. She blushed slightly thinking about it, and was surprised. She was aware Walt had a body but she always managed to keep her physical feelings under control. It was part of her determination to run her own life.

"Good-night, Melon," Angie said, giving a cheerful wave.

They were all so good-natured. Mary Ellen scowled into the darkened corridor. Even when they had nothing in particular to celebrate, they were generally on top of the world. Whereas she had deep-rooted fears that wouldn't stay in their proper places; anxieties that she wasn't doing enough, looking good enough, going far enough. All those worries kept her from really enjoying life — like Angie, for example. Now there was a saint if she ever saw one. Able to make light of a less than luxurious background, able to smile at disaster, able to go to a dance without even the promise of a date.

"I'm just different, I guess," she muttered to herself, throwing her parka over her shoulders and tugging at the front door of Tarenton High. "I'm really more like Pres — a loner." And then, for a brief second, she wished for him back again, too. "You malcontent," she grumbled into her scarf. "He's got Kerry now — leave him alone."

When she saw Donny's car, she walked toward it as though it were dangerous. And when she slipped into the passenger seat and snapped her seatbelt into place, she distinctly heard the clang of a prison door shutting in her mind. But a number one guy was what she wanted. Wasn't it?

Pres and Kerry looked at the curtains Nancy had dropped off. After that Sunday afternoon, she'd gone into a sewing frenzy, finding fabric at a flea market sale and rushing home to "create," as she called it. The curtains were bright orange with yellow flowers, and they almost reached to the bottom of the studio windows. There was only about a five-inch gap.

"What do you think?" Pres asked, examining

them as though they were some exotic species of animal.

"They sort of remind me of my grandmother's kitchen — I don't know," Kerry sighed. "They don't do much for me."

"Me, either." Gratefully, Pres started to put them back in the box.

"But she's here so often. She'd be hurt if you didn't hang them up."

"So, she'll be hurt. Kerry, they're disgusting," Pres moaned.

"I say they go up." Kerry, for all her sweetness, had opinions. Though most people saw her as kind of vague, drifting through life, that was really just a cover for her shyness. She didn't speak her mind with just anybody, but now that she felt more comfortable with Pres, she wasn't afraid to be up front with him.

"You hang them, then," he muttered, thrusting them at her. "I want nothing to do with it."

She had just begun to string them on the curtain rods when they heard the sound of a car coming up the road. Pres tensed at once.

"What's the matter?" Kerry had become an expert at sensing his mood changes.

"Nothing. It's just . . . I wasn't expecting company." He *knew* that sooner or later his father was going to come and have it out with him. There was no way that he was going to leave the situation as it was, when it was well known all over town that Preston Tilford II couldn't even keep a tight rein on his own son. If there was anything his father hated more than losing money in business, it was being thought of as a chump.

"Whose car is that?" Kerry peered out into the gathering dark.

Pres joined her at the window, noting with relief that the car parked beside the studio was a beat-up Volkswagen Beetle. His father wouldn't be caught dead in a Beetle.

There was a quick rap at the door, followed by a raucous war whoop. As Pres put his hand on the knob, the door flew open, and in crashed a tall, muscular guy with a curly red beard that scrawled all over his thin face like graffiti.

"Well, who are you?" the stranger asked.

"I'm Pres; this is Kerry."

"Pres? Not little Pres! You're kidding!" The bearded wonder extended his hand and pumped Pres's up and down for a long minute. "The last time I saw you, you didn't even know how to put your socks on straight."

Pres scowled. "A.J.?" he asked. It couldn't be anyone else.

"The one and only." The guy started giving Kerry the eye. "And what's your name, cute stuff?" He reached out for Kerry.

"This is my cousin, A.J.," Pres told Kerry quickly, stepping between them. "Just passing through, I would think." A.J. was James's only son, but they hardly knew each other. He'd lived with James's ex-wife after the divorce, but he was apparently quite a handful, and she got fed up, sending him off to boarding school somewhere in New Hampshire. Pres's mother had mentioned a few months ago that A.J. had just started at Columbia University and wasn't doing awfully well.

110

"Hey, you living here now?" A.J. dropped his leather carryall and plunked himself down on the couch.

"Yeah, I am," Pres said a little defensively.

"You don't mind if I crash here for a while, do you? I'm kind of on leave from college, if you know what I mean." He winked at Kerry.

"James is out of town for a couple of days at a show, but I'm sure it would be okay if you stayed in the main house," Pres told him. "He left me a key." He dug down deep in his pocket and produced it, then tossed it to his cousin who let it fall on the floor in front of him.

"Oh, hey, that's cool. Really. But, honey, I still don't know your name."

"It's Kerry. Pres, I think I better be getting home," she said, clearly uncomfortable with this boy whose thoughts were obvious.

"Want a ride?" A.J. asked. "I've been driving for eight hours straight — might as well keep going."

"That's okay," Kerry smiled as nicely as she could. "Pres, let's move it, shall we?" She tossed her jacket over her shoulder and was out the door without even saying good-bye.

"So, I guess I'll see you whenever," Pres told A.J. firmly.

"I'll be out by the time you get back. Just have to shut my eyes a sec, okay?" A.J. yawned widely, then put his boots up on the couch and lay back.

Pres drove Kerry home slowly. He was not looking forward to finding his cousin right where he'd left him — and knowing A.J., he probably

111

hadn't made an attempt to move and wasn't going to for the rest of the night.

"You two don't have much in common, do you?" Kerry asked when Pres had been silent for ten minutes or so.

"Not a whole lot. He always goes home to his mother in Virginia. I don't remember when James last saw him. They never got along."

"I can see why."

"Well, I'll get him out of the studio tomorrow. Wonder how long he intends to stick around Tarenton." He didn't think James would evict him from the studio, but if he really couldn't stand having A.J. under the same roof with him, that would mean it was share or move out. And *then* what was Pres going to do? He couldn't go home. But he doubted that he could stay in the same space as his cousin for very long without starting a fist fight.

"See you in school, okay? Sleep well," Kerry told him as he pulled up in front of her house. He leaned over and kissed her gently, feeling her warmth creeping over him and into him. Their kisses were gentle to begin with, soft and whispery. He hugged her rounded shoulders, enjoying her curves against his leanness. Then he kissed her harder and pulled her closer.

With a sigh, before Pres's hands could move from her shoulders, she reached back and opened the door. Then she was gone, and he was alone.

"Why won't you let me come with you? Hey, I'm not gonna bother anyone," A.J. assured Pres early the next morning. Pres had made himself

112

a cup of instant coffee, and his cousin was looking at it covetously.

"Look, I gotta go," Pres said, grabbing his books and starting for the door. He purposely poured the dregs down the drain so A.J. couldn't drink them.

"I can't believe you're still going to school," A.J. shook his head in disbelief. "You have your own place, your own sexy little girl, everything copacetic, but you trudge off to Tarenton High like a good little doobie — don't even want to be late." He laughed scornfully.

Pres kept his temper, but just barely. "A.J., I'd really appreciate it if you were out by the time I get back this afternoon. We'll probably get along much better if you're in the house and I stay here. And keep away from Kerry, too."

"Hey, man, don't give it a thought. Don't you worry your little head." And with that, he turned over on the couch and went right back to sleep.

Pres wasn't concentrating awfully hard that morning. There was a spot quiz in first-period math that he totally blanked out on, and history was nearly as bad. Five of the kids were asked to sit in a circle and discuss the coming of the Industrial Revolution for the whole class — and Pres was one of the lucky ones who got picked. He said something off the wall about winning the revolution with guns instead of bows and arrows, and everyone in the room cracked up.

By lunchtime, he was ready to give it up and go home. He wandered into the cafeteria, looking for Kerry, but couldn't find her. Swarms of kids

113

were hitting the steam table at the same time, so he grabbed a sandwich and a container of milk and took a seat with some of the football jocks and their girls at a table near the window. What was he going to do, anyway? He didn't really like living alone, yet he couldn't own up to that. But A.J. could ruin everything by *forcing* him to move out. And he hated being off the squad. He itched to move again, his body doing mental gymnastics at every game he watched. He could see himself in a stag leap, or carrying Olivia on his shoulders, or swirling Mary Ellen and Angie each on an arm. He could *feel* it.

There was another problem, too, and it was getting a lot worse. Pres was out of cash. He had barely enough for groceries now, even though Kerry had been chipping in. He hated taking money from her. How ironic that the richest kid in school didn't have two cents to rub together — his father had seen to that. But then, Preston Tilford II had always been tight with a buck. He'd made it clear, when he apportioned his son's allowance, that if he wanted more, he could earn it by working at Tarenton Fabricators. Pres didn't want it that badly.

He'd been out of the house for three weeks now, and he had just about polished off the cash he'd had. He hated the idea, but soon he was going to have to dip into his savings account. He knew that as soon as he did that, his father would put a stop on it — on the whole deal. Because it was a joint account, old dad knew when things were moving over at the bank. He made it his business to know.

"Well, a free seat — exactly my size!" Vanessa's throaty sounds were so close to Pres's ear, he could hear them over the cafeteria din. "And then Goldilocks sat down in the baby bear's chair to cozy up to the big bad wolf. How're you doin', Wolf?" Her tone was blatantly suggestive — there was no doubt in Pres's mind what she was after.

"What's going on, Vannie?" he asked, as casually as he could under the circumstances.

She pulled the chair up and sat so that they were touching. He could feel her leg under her tight skirt right through his jeans.

"Just wondering how long you're going to stay out of the action. I've missed you. Where is that girl you usually hang around with, anyhow? What's her name — Kelly something?"

"I've got as much action as I want, Van," Pres said decisively, balling up the sandwich wrapper in a tight fist. "But thanks for asking."

"You keep me in mind if things get dull, all right?" she told him.

He was on his feet and moving away from the table when he spotted the one person who could rattle him faster than Vanessa. With a grunt, he waited as A.J. approached their table.

"Hey, little cousin, I found you! How's the school trip today?" A.J. asked, his eyes all over Vanessa. She was asking for the attention, and she got it.

"Hello," she sparkled at him. "I'm Vanessa Barlow, your welcoming committee at Tarenton High. And whom do I have the pleasure of welcoming?"

"A.J. Tilford, Pres's cousin, just in from New York for a visit." His deep-set gray eyes narrowed a little, sizing her up. "I didn't think I was going to stay long, but now I might."

Vanessa gave him one of her slow, lingering smiles, and flung her dark hair invitingly over one shoulder. "You live in New York?"

"Temporarily. Officially, I'm at Columbia, but my real reason for being there is to attend the New York City University of Life. The street action's really wild, if you know what I mean."

"Of course," she said. A.J. had just risen several notches in her estimation. Not only was he a college man, but he was above and beyond organized education. The pirate king, the highwayman robber amidst all these dumb high school boys.

"You free for lunch?" A.J. asked her. "And I don't mean this garbage," he scoffed, indicating the unappealing food strewn over every table.

"I sure am." Vanessa was on her feet and moving toward the door instantly. She looked back once to make certain that A.J. was following her, and caught Pres's eye. "You don't mind, do you?" she asked him.

"Hey, Van, I think you two deserve each other. Have a great time," he added sarcastically.

As Pres watched them go out of the cafeteria, it struck him that despite his various and multifaceted problems, he wasn't that bad off. He might be lonely, he might be off the cheerleading team, he might have money troubles, but at least he wasn't a creep. And that was more than could be said for a lot of people.

CHAPTER

"Oh, no, he's early," Olivia moaned, looking out the window at the Jeep parked at an angle in the drive. "Now he'll get stuck with my mother!"

Hurriedly, she splashed on some cologne, then started on her makeup. Olivia generally didn't put much on her face at all, except for moisturizer, but tonight was special. And besides, she needed something to bring out the luscious lavender color of her new angora sweater with the pink pearl buttons along the side of the neck. She dabbed on some gleaming brown shadow, then outlined the crease of her eye with a soft lavender pencil. A little blusher, a little pink lip gloss, and she was ready. She just prayed her new shoes wouldn't cause too many blisters. After all, she had practice on Monday, and self-imposed blisters from wearing the wrong footgear were definitely frowned upon by Ardith. She whizzed down the stairs, jumping the last three. There he was, cornered.

"Hi, Walt. 'Bye, Mom. We won't be too late." If she could just whisk them out of there without a scene!

"I was just telling Walter, dear, that smoke-filled rooms make it difficult for you to breathe. No one smokes at that school of yours, do they?"

Olivia gave Walt a look. "Oh, no, Mom, they wouldn't dream of it. Shall we go?"

Mrs. Evans rose to her full height, glaring at the two of them. She wasn't tall, but her broad shoulders and hips gave her a massive presence. She wasn't the kind of person you'd feel comfortable meeting in a dark alley.

"I want you to know, Walter, that my daughter is still very frail. This strange break dancing and disco junk is strictly inadvisable. Do you understand?"

"I certainly do, Mrs. Evans," Walt said seriously, before Olivia could jump in with a sarcastic comment. "We will confine ourselves to very slow moonwalking." And with that, he swept up his jacket and Olivia's coat from the hall rack and steered his date outside. She was nearly convulsed with giggles as they got to the car.

"You're a riot, you know that?" She laughed as he took the time to kiss her forehead, then her nose, and finally, her inviting lips.

"Oh, is that it? And your mother led me to believe that I *cause* riots. Let's hit the road, kid!"

They were off, driving through the still, chilly night. Tarenton dances were generally big events,

118

and tonight's was no exception. The kids on the entertainment committee always provided the best decorations, the hottest DJ, and some really good refreshments. They were only able to manage the finances by asking all comers to donate at the door, of course, and though some kids objected to this, they all gave. It was a tradition.

"There's Angie's car," Walt commented, as they pulled into the already crowded school parking lot and he turned off the ignition. "Did she come alone?"

"She said her brother Andrew was taking her. Didn't seem very broken up about it, though," Olivia said. "I think she has her eye on somebody who promised to be here," she added mysteriously.

"Who?"

"Wouldn't you like to know? Buy me a Coke and maybe I'll tell."

Laughing, they ran into the building. All the lights on the upper floors were blazing, and the chaperones were standing around the front hallway, waiting for enough kids to show so that the dance could start.

"Door prizes? No, thanks. Hey, I never win anything." Josh was standing with his arm around Nancy at the entrance to the gym, as Walt and Olivia approached. A senior with thick glasses and a very serious expression was trying to convince everyone who entered to sign up for a prize. That meant extra admission, of course.

"What's the prize?" Nancy wanted to know. Her cheeks were flushed, nearly matching the deep red of her silk vest. Under it, she wore a

119

white silk blouse with billowing sleeves.

"I don't know," the senior told her.

"Well, if you don't know, who does?"

"I have an inkling." It was Pres. As he strolled up to the gym door with Kerry on his arm, he looked happier than he had in weeks. He leaned over and whispered in Nancy's ear, then did the same to Kerry, who gave him a dubious look, then shook her head. "Old exam books with answers in them, huh? Doesn't sound too exciting to me. Not tonight, anyhow." She looked so proud, so sophisticated, as Pres escorted her inside the noisy gym.

"In that case, fella," Josh said to the disgruntled senior, "I'll just take two regular tickets. And two for my friend, Walt."

The gym looked magical tonight — nothing like the sweaty arena they worked out in every day, although the smell still hung on. There were Mylar balloons everywhere, and Japanese paper lanterns over the old hanging light fixtures to dim the glare a little. The walls had been plastered with rock album covers, and a miniature stage had been set up under one of the baskets for the disc jockey. He was a college kid, dressed all in black leather, with unbelievable hair. Nancy didn't know whether to watch his yellow-and-green-streaked concoction bobbing in time to the music or Pres dancing with Kerry.

"Place looks terrific!" Josh said, sweeping Nancy into a fast twirling pattern on the floor. He certainly had style, Nancy thought. She didn't always feel that she was the lightest person on her feet, but Josh made her feel positively ethereal.

Mary Ellen and Donny walked in next, saying rather subdued hellos to the other two couples. Olivia caught Mary Ellen's eye, but she looked away. One thing was certain — she wasn't delirious about being here. Or was it being with Donny that was upsetting her? Although she looked lovely in a soft blue-gray velveteen top and tight-fitting jeans, her mind was clearly elsewhere. And her eyes scanned the floor hungrily. Olivia was certain she was looking for Patrick. The thing was, if Patrick was here, *he* would find *her*, Donny or no Donny.

"Hello, everybody! Party time!" Vanessa's deep voice made everyone turn suddenly, their light moods darkened somewhat by the appearance of one of their least favorite people. "Do you know my date? A.J. Tilford, this is the rah-rah crew — you know, those cheerleaders your little cousin Pres used to associate with. And this is A.J., guys, direct from New York City." She spoke quickly, looking around the floor instead of at them. She wanted to make sure everyone was suitably impressed with the big fish she'd snagged.

"Oh, is that Angie?" Vanessa continued, peering out into the corridor. "Poor little Angie had to come all by herself. I really feel for her," she sighed in exaggerated concern.

"And we really feel for you, Vanessa," Walt said quietly, starting toward Angie before she could hear any of this.

"So that makes it even," Olivia called over her

shoulder. She caught up to Walt and whispered, "Ask Angie to dance. Go on. I'll go grab some food so I can tell you what's good."

He beamed at her, loving her for her generosity, her open spirit. And then, before Angie could even say hello, she felt herself whisked through the door of the gym, onto the crowded floor. The senior at the door waved at them, but there was nothing he could do. Walt and Angie were moving too fast for him, doing double pirouettes and fancy lifts to the wild music.

Olivia watched them for a second, then wandered to the refreshment table. A.J. Tilford had fixed himself a large plate of pizza, chips, and dip, and was leaning back, blocking the table from Olivia's view. She walked around him, then grabbed a glass of Coke.

"Vanessa went to the little girls' room," he said without further preliminaries. "You want to. . . ?" He moved his finger in a circle, indicating dancing.

"Ah, not really. Thanks. I'll sit this one out," Olivia nodded.

"Not much to get excited about, right? Hey, this place is a drag already. But in a podunk town, with a podunk high school, what can you expect?"

He was so smug, she wanted to smack him. "Oh, and I suppose it's just *fantastic* in New York City." Her small body fairly bristled with rage.

"Are you kidding? Babe, school dances are really out. I mean, we're talking *tired blood*, you

122

know what I mean? You want to split?" He looked at her through dull gray eyes. The odd thing was, he didn't seem to care whether she said yes or no.

So she said neither. She put down her glass and simply walked away toward the ladies' room. If Vanessa wasn't out of there by now, she'd just ignore her. All she knew was that it was important to put as much distance as possible between herself and this big hairy ape.

There was someone in the ladies' room, but it wasn't Vanessa. Mary Ellen was standing in front of one of the sinks, splashing water on her face and gulping air. It was evident that she had been crying.

"Hey, it's too early to fall apart. The dance has hardly begun," Oilvia said. "What's going on?" When Mary Ellen just shook her head, Olivia crossed her arms and looked at her through the mirror. "It's Vanessa, right? She was in here and said something horrible."

"Sort of. Not really. It's not important." Mary Ellen sniffed, her breath coming in shuddery jerks as she tried to calm herself down. It was all coming to a head, and for some reason, she just wasn't coping very well anymore. She knew it was dumb to believe anything Vanessa said, but somehow, with things going bad with Donny and her own mixed-up emotions, anything seemed possible. There was something so logical about what Vanessa had told her — that Angie had come to the dance specifically to see Patrick. "Isn't that sweet?" she'd gushed on her way out the door. She loved to drop megaton bombs, then waltz away just before everything crashed around her.

But Mary Ellen wasn't going to let this news spoil her evening. She had to be happy and cheerful — everyone expected it of her. "Hey, we better get back." She tried a laugh, but it sounded hollow to Olivia. "How do I look?"

"You always look beautiful," said the ever-practical Olivia. She didn't believe in getting overly emotional about anything, so she didn't press Mary Ellen for an answer. All she said was, "Watch out for Vanessa's date, by the way. He's perfectly awful, and seems to want to go home with the first girl who looked bored or unhappy. You, Melon, are a prime target."

"I'll be careful," Mary Ellen promised, taking a deep breath. The music swirled over them as they walked back onto the floor. It was loud enough to vibrate in their stomachs, and the dancing was crazy enough to get lost in. They stood to one side, scouting the territory, and then Olivia spotted Walt looking for her and edged her way toward him. That left Mary Ellen standing alone.

She'd never been a wallflower in her life. It felt weird. And yet, she wasn't surprised that Donny didn't want to dance with her. She'd been making things pretty tough for him lately, and as soon as they'd entered the gym, he'd gravitated right to his basketball buddies, some of whom hadn't come with dates. She could see him now, going over a tough pass he wanted to use at the game next week. His pal Hank took the imaginary ball from him and feinted to his right, nearly knocking over a couple who were swaying together on the dance floor.

"Why so glum, lady?" Pres saw her moping there and dragged Kerry and Angie over to her corner.

"I'm not!" Mary Ellen protested much too cheerily. "How are you guys doing? Great music, isn't it?" She was wound too tight, talking too fast. No one believed her for a minute.

"How about a dance?" Pres asked her, half turning to Kerry for permission. She smiled and motioned them both toward the floor.

"If you don't mind, I think I'll pass. I didn't sleep very well last night and I'm kinda beat." Her eyes were focused straight ahead of her, on Patrick's strong, broad back. He was hopping around with two girls, a couple of juniors Mary Ellen didn't know very well. She told herself to stay where she was — if he wanted her, he'd find her.

"Okay, but you're missing the chance of a lifetime," Pres cautioned her. "Kerry?"

"Nope. I've had it — for a while, anyway. Angie, it's up to you. I'll be over there with my shoes off. Have fun!"

Pres shrugged, then pushed Angie onto the floor before she could bow out. The DJ switched turntables, and a slow number boomed from the huge speakers. Angie moved closer, and Pres put his arms around her protectively, steering her in a tight circle. She was the one girl he could hug without any mixed feelings. She was a friend, and touching her was just nice — not a sexual invitation. He had never, for one minute, been turned on by Angie.

"How are you and your cousin working out together?" she asked solicitously, lifting her blonde head from his shoulder.

"We avoid each other, period," Pres laughed. "He moved into the main house after I told him for the tenth time, but he threatens to come back to the studio when Uncle James gets home tomorrow. And the worst part is, I don't know how long A.J. intends to stay. Looks like he's getting very comfortable."

"So what'll you do if he crowds you out?" Angie looked deep into his eyes, demanding honesty from him. She liked Pres a lot — always had — and she hated to see him do dumb things. "Have you considered moving back home?"

Pres rolled his eyes up to the ceiling, then spun her under his arm. "No lectures or I drop you right here. Just dance, will you, please?"

"Don't you avoid me, Pres." Angie stopped in the middle of the floor and took him by the hand. "Don't you dare. I want you back on our squad, and this is the only way I'm going to get you."

"What's wrong with Mr. Wonderful?" He jerked his head over at Josh and Nancy, who were locked in a close embrace, swaying slowly on a dime-sized spot on the floor.

"Nothing. He's good, perfect sometimes. But he isn't part of our team and never will be. He doesn't mesh the way you do. We all feel it, even though no one's talking about it — partly not to hurt Nancy's feelings. She's pretty gone on the guy."

126

"I can see. Hey, could we talk about this some other time? I have to *move*, Ange." He did a few snazzy dance steps in place, feeling itchy all over. Other people could talk to him about this subject, and he'd just laugh it off. But Angie was different. She looked deeper inside him than anyone, except maybe Kerry, who was always on his side. But Angie didn't pull any punches. She said what she thought.

"You want to move; I want to stand still for a second. Who wins? I can't talk and dance at the same time."

He sighed, then nodded reluctantly. They fought their way off the dance floor and walked past the refreshment table, over to the big windows that faced the back of the school. It was about a hundred decibels quieter here, which was not saying a great deal.

"Why won't you move back home, Pres?" Angie demanded, her clear blue eyes like a beacon in the huge room. "You've been away for weeks now. Wouldn't this be a perfect time to make peace with your folks, particularly since you have that unwelcomed visitor hanging around?"

"No time is a perfect time, Ange. Yeah, I know, sooner or later I'm going to have to bite the bullet. If only. . . ." He let the thought trail off.

"It's your dad, isn't it? Have you talked to him?"

"No, just to my mother. She wasn't a lot of help. I don't think Preston Tilford II really *wants* me back. I mean, talk about a laissez-faire policy! The man's oblivious to me. I might as well not

127

even be there." He balled up his fists. Just the thought of his father made him want to hit something.

"Pres, I don't know your parents. But even if you aren't crazy about the guy, he's the only father you've got. I may sound like a sap, but that's my opinion, for what it's worth."

He looked at the floor, then out at the dancers, slick now with sweat and the excitement of the pulsing beat. They were all so *normal*, with their normal families and normal school activities and normal boyfriends and girl friends. And he was such a misfit. Except that Angie didn't think so. She was a rock, no doubt about it. He put his arms around her and squeezed hard, taking her completely by surprise.

"You really want me back, huh?"

"Do I!"

"Well, I'll think about it." He let her go, a little nervous about hugging somebody who wasn't Kerry right in sight of everybody. Kerry wouldn't blink, because it was Angie — but a lot of other people might start some nasty rumors. They had before.

"Look, I've got to go rescue Kerry from the chorus line over there. See you later." He was smiling as he walked her over to her brother and ducked away, over to the line of chairs against the wall. Angie gave the V for victory sign behind his back.

"Are you ready to dance yet?" Pres demanded as he swept Kerry up off her feet. "Because it's either that or I do a loony number by myself. I've got to blow off some steam, lady!"

"You're on," she murmured, stepping away from Mary Ellen, who'd been standing beside Kerry's chair for the past ten minutes.

"We'll be back when we fall down, Melon," Pres called to her, but she didn't hear him. Patrick was walking directly toward her, tall and determined and giving her that wide, lopsided grin that never failed to turn her insides to the consistency of hot oatmeal.

He didn't ask her to dance; he simply took both her hands and drew her toward him. They weren't on the dance floor, but suddenly, they were swaying together, their fingers interlaced, their bodies brushing with tantalizing eagerness.

And for the first time in a long time, Mary Ellen didn't give him a fight. She let herself be drawn forward, let her head drop heavily onto the front of his chest; let her eyes close dreamily as he led her in a small, slow circle. They might have been the only people in the room. As for Donny, she had no idea where he was, nor did she care.

"You smell so good," Patrick said at last, whispering below the sonic boom of the record. "I'm going to remember this smell when I go to sleep tonight."

She turned her head to him, looking into his dark eyes, feeling the wall of his muscles surrounding and encasing her.

"Kiss me, would you, Patrick?" she asked softly. It didn't matter that they were in the middle of the Tarenton High gym; it didn't even matter that the guy she'd come in with was somewhere nearby. Nor did it matter that she'd promised herself not to let Patrick get any closer than a room's length away. Tonight, she needed some security, some place of her own. And he wanted her — despite what Vanessa had said, she could sense it. He'd always wanted her.

His wavy forelock dipped over his right eyebrow as he stooped and placed his lips on hers. They were warm and wonderfully slow and easy on her anxious mouth. He simply let them both enjoy the moment, touching her gently. Their movement stopped completely, and for a moment, they were suspended in time.

"Just what the hell do you think you're doing?!" In the next instant, their contact was rudely broken. Mary Ellen felt Patrick wrenched out of her arms, and then she saw Donny. His face was red. There was no emotion in his eyes at all.

"We were dancing," Patrick said quietly. "Since you haven't danced with her all night, I figured she might be bored. Might be bored even if you *had* been paying attention to her," he chuckled.

Donny's arm was a steel piston, ready to pump. As Mary Ellen screamed, Walt, Hank Vreewright, and three other guys from the basketball team jumped on top of Donny, holding him off, but just barely.

"I'll fight for her, if you want to," Patrick told him brusquely. "But wouldn't it be more sensible just to ask her whether that's necessary?"

"Aw, who cares?" Donny spat at Mary Ellen, as he shook the guys off him angrily. "This thing's been over for weeks now. I'm glad to get her off my back. But you, mister," he growled at Patrick, "you just better stay out of my way." And with that, he stalked off, the muscles in the back of his neck bunched like a mass of granite.

The chaperones, too late to stop the fight, were busy trying to restore order on the floor and get the dance going again. The other kids were buzzing about the commotion, which made Mary Ellen feel exposed and bruised. Patrick's arm circled her protectively, and he tried to walk her away from the main action, but it was difficult. She was still the center of attention. Yes, it was true she'd wanted to end the relationship with Donny, but why did it have to be like this, in front of everyone? She could *feel* Vanessa smirking at her all the way across the room.

"Are you okay?" Pres was at her side in a second.

"Sure." She smiled weakly at him, then turned to Patrick. "You better take me home."

"Your wish is my command." Patrick, through the whole thing, had been cool as ice. He'd come to the dance with one purpose — to take Mary Ellen home — and now that she'd asked him to, he didn't need to preen or make a fuss.

"We're leaving, too," said Angie, who'd dragged her brother Andrew over as soon as she'd seen Donny march out of the gym. She took Mary Ellen aside for a moment. "I never could stand that overblown beanpole. He shoots a mean basket, but the rest of him is all over the court, if you know what I mean."

Mary Ellen nodded glumly, grateful for the support but still furious with herself for causing all this ruckus.

"I think I've had it, too, Pres," Kerry sighed. "Do you mind?"

"No, it's fine." He scanned the floor for Vanessa and A.J., but couldn't see them. Luckily, he'd managed to avoid them all night, and that was certainly okay with him.

Josh and Nancy, and Walt and Olivia were still dancing, still so wrapped up in one another that it would have been a shame to stop them to say good-night. Mary Ellen let Patrick help her into her jacket, and together, they walked steadily out of the gym, past the small crowd of gawkers, and down to the parking lot. Only the feeling of his hand holding hers kept her going. She didn't know whether this was going to be a turning point in her life or a night she'd regret as long as she lived.

She let Patrick help her up into the cab of his garbage truck and waved down at Pres, who was helping Kerry climb into the Porsche. The contrast might have amused her at some other time, but now, nothing seemed awfully funny.

"I love you, Mary Ellen. I hope you know that," Patrick said solemnly as he put his key in the ignition.

"I do. I've known for a long time." It wasn't much of an answer — she knew that — but it was all she could manage now. She didn't know how to deal with Patrick's love — how to accept it, enjoy it, and not let it take over her life.

CHAPTER

"You can't tell me you didn't have a wonderful time." Josh softly stroked the hair out of Nancy's face and let his hand rest for a moment on her cool cheek. They stood together on the porch of her house, listening to the wind and to each other.

"No, I can't tell you that," she admitted.

"And you can't deny that you and I really hit it off together," he persisted.

"All right, I give. We're a match. Good-night, Josh," she laughed gently, her hand on the doorknob.

"Nancy, you forgot something." He turned her around again, taking her by the shoulders. He was still smiling, but there was an intensity behind the grin that cancelled out any thought of laughter.

She could see herself reflected in his dark eyes, and feel herself melting. They drew closer, and then their bodies touched. She wrapped her arms around his neck and inhaled the sharp soap smell of him. He hugged her to him, his small, muscular form insisting on the kiss, holding her, demanding her response.

Just as their lips separated, the front door was pulled open. Nancy jumped so far away from him, she might have been executing a particularly difficult cheering maneuver. Her heart was going as if she'd run a mile.

"Oh, dear, I'm so sorry!" Her mother stood there in the dark, her robe wrapped around her. She ran her fingers nervously around the base of her neck. "I heard voices but no one was coming in and I just thought . . . oh, I'm really sorry!"

"What's going on?" Nancy's father, looking rumpled from sleep, stood behind her in his pajamas. "Is everything all right?"

"Yes, certainly, dear. Let's just get back to bed and let these two young people say good-night." Mrs. Goldstein, to her credit, remembered what it was like to come home from a dance and have your parents hovering in the background like hungry wolves about to pounce.

"I'll be right in, Mother," Nancy said softly. Had they seen Josh? He was hanging back, out of the dim glow of the porch light.

"You know, sweetie," her father said as he turned his back on them, "it's not against the house rules to invite the gentleman in for some hot cocoa. Except I guess you kids don't drink cocoa nowadays. Oh well, good-night."

There was a muffled chortle from the dark side of the porch. Josh had started to laugh and couldn't stop himself. Nancy looked despairingly in his direction, but it was too late. Her parents had already noticed his bush of dark hair and heard his distinctive laugh.

"Josh? Josh Breitman? Is that you?" Mrs. Goldstein took a step toward him. "Why Nancy, you never. . . ." She looked from one to the other, incredulous.

"Hi, Mrs. Goldstein, Mr. Goldstein." Josh walked into the light, coming over to shake each of their hands. "Nice to see you again."

"But Nancy, you always told us that. . . ." Her father rubbed his chin, then his thinning hair. "I will never in a million years understand teenagers," he muttered as he rubbed his eyes. "Say, it's awfully cold out here. Could everyone please come inside?"

"Josh, it's so wonderful to see you," Mrs. Goldstein said. Nancy wanted to crawl under the porch.

"Uh, Nancy, I don't know if I should really come in right now. I kind of said I'd be home at a respectable hour — and it's been past 'respectable' for hours."

Mrs. Goldstein sighed happily, relishing the very idea of a seventeen-year-old boy who did what his parents asked. "Of course. Well, we'll see you soon, I hope. Good-night, dear." She pushed her husband back inside and closed the door. Josh and Nancy could hear them on the other side, laughing.

"You're sunk now," Josh said to her quietly. "Cat out of bag; boyfriend's cover blown."

Nancy tried to look mad, but she couldn't. The

135

whole thing was too funny. "Did you see the expressions on their faces? I love it when I completely blow their minds." She giggled, then roared.

"Now you'll never get rid of me," Josh said happily, leaning over to kiss her nose. "They won't let you."

"That'll be my decision, mister. Now, get out of here."

He kissed her again, a soft brush of the lips that grew deeper as they stood there. She pulled away after a long time, breathless, craving more. Still, she couldn't help thinking of her parents somewhere on the other side of the door. It sort of put a damper on her ardor. "Call me tomorrow," she whispered as she ducked inside.

Josh Breitman could have flown home. But since he had the car with him, he decided he might as well drive.

"You're sure you want to go home alone?" Andrew Poletti looked at Angie through the open car window.

"Don't worry about me. You guys go get your ice cream sundaes and have a great time," Angie told him cheerily.

"But I've never known you to pass up ice cream before," her brother persisted. "You sure you're not sick?"

"I'm not sick — just feeling slightly flabby around the middle these days. You know, I have to at least try to stay normal-sized for cheering. Honest, that's the real reason. Now will you get out of here? They're waiting for you."

And indeed, as Andrew looked over toward the Ford pickup his pal Sonny was driving, the horn honked and eight kids yelled at him to get a move on. He shrugged and looked at her again. "Okay, tell Mom I'll be home in an hour." He started to walk away, then came back to her.

"What is it now?" She waggled a finger at him.

"Did you have a good time tonight?"

"I had a wonderful time," Angie asserted, "and a wonderful date. But now, I wish he'd get lost." Without further ado, she turned the key in the ignition and started off briskly, so he wouldn't have the chance to come back and bug her again.

She didn't really want to go home, and yet, there was nowhere else she really wanted to go, either, so she figured she might as well call it a night. The odd thing was, she'd been boyfriendless before, and it had never gotten to her at all. She could go to a school dance by herself and have a ball and never think twice about the fact that she was going to end the evening without a good-night kiss, without so much as a friendly handshake. So why was tonight different?

Maybe it was seeing everyone she cared about matched up, even Walt and Olivia, for heaven's sake — and Walt had never been attached with anyone before. Maybe it was realizing, after her talk with Pres, how precious the fundamentals were. Of course, of all her friends, and certainly of all the guys on the team, she had the best family, hands down. Her mom and brothers kept her on target — they really cared deeply about what happened to her — and that was about as fundamental as you could get.

She missed Marc. She couldn't deny that. But she couldn't be expected to get over him within one month. She tried not to look back, not to feel sorry for herself. But something else was bothering her, and she would just have to forget it. That something was Patrick Henley.

What difference did it make if she'd recently been having lunch at his table, or going over her lab notes with him, or even walking from fifth to sixth period with him? None whatsoever. Because he was so stuck on Mary Ellen that other girls were merely background noise as far as he was concerned. And it was true that Angie and Patrick had never been more than good friends, whereas he and Melon had had this love-hate thing going for over a year now.

There were other guys she could date, and some of them really liked her. If Angie set her mind to it (except that she hated the idea of purposely going out to snag a boyfriend), she could probably go out with any one of half a dozen guys on a regular basis. Did she just develop this thing for Patrick because she knew he was unavailable? Was she that crazy?

She sighed as she pulled the car into the driveway and parked. Nothing was so bad, really. Nothing that was going to hurt so terribly in the long run. But tonight, she felt wistful. The thing of it was, she was happy that Melon had finally gotten rid of Donny. Could you be happy for someone else, and also a little mad at her because she had something you wanted, all at the same time?

"Home so early?" Rose Poletti was sitting in

front of the TV, knitting, when her daughter came in. "Turn that thing off, will you? I'm not even watching it. How was the dance? Did you have a good time? And where's your brother?"

"Don't be a worrywart," Angie cautioned her, kissing her on the top of her head. "Dance was fine; Andrew's out with the gang. I'm going to bed. See you in the A.M."

She was on her way up the stairs when she heard her mother say, "Dancing must be harder than cheerleading. You look pooped."

"Just a bit. I'll sleep well tonight."

And she would, too, if she could just resign herself to the fact that Patrick and Mary Ellen were now a unit. That was that.

Pres and Kerry sat in the Porsche for a good half hour and talked. He didn't tell her what Angie had said, nor what he'd vaguely promised her. He had to chew on that for a while, had to see how it fit in his scheme of things.

So instead, they covered all the likely topics: how crazy they were about each other (capped by a kiss), Mary Ellen's problem with guys, Walt and Olivia, Josh and Nancy, A.J. and how awful he was, and how crazy they were about each other (capped by another, longer kiss). It was after midnight when they said good-night and Pres reluctantly put the car in gear. He would have loved to have driven Kerry right back to the studio, made a fire, and curled up with her in front of it. He thought about going further than that. He thought about it a lot, but she was too young and anyhow, sex might mess up the great thing they had going. What Kerry gave him was more than just physical thrills. She gave him part of her soul.

He drove slowly, savoring the quiet. Tarenton couldn't have been called busy at any time of day, (technically, there *was* a rush hour, except that it was only ten minutes long), but at night the town was like an empty shell, waiting to be filled. Pres loved the feeling of having it all to himself. The road was his, and he could drive as fast or as slow as he wanted. The big maples and sycamores were his, the bare branches arching over the narrow highways. And the night sounds were his, too — the scurry of a startled rabbit, the brisk wind, the creak of a cracked tree limb. Driving at night in Tarenton made Pres peaceful, as he never could be during the day.

He was cruising along, about fifty yards from his destination, when he noticed the smoke coming out of the studio's chimney. He *always* let the fire die down before he left the place — that was one thing he'd promised James. The answer was plain and neat: A.J. was ensconced again. And the lights were out, which meant that the louse had plopped down on the couch and gone to sleep, damn him.

With a set jaw, Pres parked and stalked up to the studio door. He stuck his key in the lock and turned it, but nothing happened. What was going on? He never double-locked this place — there wasn't any reason to. He turned the key around again and the door moved under his hand. But he didn't move. He didn't like what he heard inside.

"A.J.," he stated firmly in a loud voice.

Silence. He took a step into the room. Then he heard a covered whisper, and throaty, muffled laughter.

"Look, whatever you're doing in here, you better can it." He felt like a jerk, talking to the dark room.

Then he heard two feet hit the floor and the shuffling sound of someone coming toward him. The red beard looked lopsided in the pitch dark.

"What's going on, A.J.?" Pres asked indignantly. "I thought you said you'd stay in the main house."

"Sure, little cousin. I am. It's just a lot cozier in here, with the fire and all. Here, why don't you take the key back and *you* stay in the house tonight?"

Pres took the proffered key and peered at A.J. suspiciously. He was bare-chested and barefooted, and even in the backlight of the woodstove, he could tell that the guy was looking pretty smug.

"What'd you double-lock the door for?" Pres asked. He knew there was something going on, and he intended to find out. Then he intended to get his studio back and throw the guy out.

"Can't a man have any privacy?" A.J. asked. "Listen, good buddy, I'd really like to continue this conversation some other time if that's okay with you. I've, uh, kind of got something going here, get it? So how about you get lost for a few hours?"

Pres took a step into the room. He could now make out another form on the couch, and it

141

was female. "Sorry," Pres said staunchly. "Hate to break up the party, but she'll have to go. House rules. I told Uncle James there wouldn't be any overnight dates on the premises." He couldn't believe himself, acting so responsible. And it wasn't even his problem, strictly speaking.

"Boy, are you a party pooper," said a familiar husky voice from the vicinity of the couch. "Pres, we were just making out, nothing more serious than that — so far." Vanessa lifted herself up on one arm, and Pres could see in the firelight that she still had all her clothes on, although they'd been sort of rearranged.

"I said out." Pres felt perfectly wonderful about destroying Vanessa's good time.

A.J. sighed and padded back to the couch, where he helped himself to the cigarettes lying on the end table. He lit two at once and handed one to Vanessa, which she held out before her like the Statue of Liberty brandishing her torch.

"I've put up with a lot from you, A.J.," Pres continued. "But I told your father I'd see to it that nothing got out of hand here."

"Nothing's out of hand, little cousin. Vanessa and I just have this date, see?"

"Not in the studio you don't. And not in the main house either. Why don't you take her home to the Barlow residence and see what the superintendent of the Tarenton schools has to say about it?"

A.J. frowned, then looked over at Vanessa, who suddenly seemed very bored. "C'mon, honey," he said to her, throwing a couple of shoes

142

in her direction. "Somebody has just rained on our parade. Let's adjourn to the car."

"It's too cold in the car," Vanessa whined. Then she shrugged and stood up, rearranging her clothing precisely, making Pres watch. "You might as well take me home — now that he's spoiled everything."

Taking their time, the two of them gathered their things and sauntered to the door of the studio. Pres didn't move; he didn't say another word. He'd gotten his message across and he was oddly proud of himself. It was weird — when he was living with his parents, and before he met Kerry, he would have done just what A.J. was doing. A strange girl in a strange place. Tonight, though, he felt older and in control of the situation.

"Good-night," Vanessa growled at him as A.J. ushered her out the door.

"Hey, little buddy, I'll need that key to the main house back, now that you've evicted me." A.J. held out his hand, and Pres just let it hang there in mid-air.

"Key? That's funny, I thought I had it here somewhere." He pretended to search his pockets. "Must have lost it. I guess that means you sleep in the car tonight, *good buddy*." He closed the door on them, double-locked it, then leaned against it for good measure. There was nothing wrong with being a mean son-of-a-gun every once in a while, he thought. As he got ready for bed, he whistled a little tune, then threw another log on the fire.

CHAPTER

The six cheerleaders ran in a line, then physically threw themselves forward, cartwheeling their way across the floor. When they reached the other end of the gym, they repeated the move, but this time, they each added a back flip and a straddle jump before turning into the amazing whirling dervishes. Back again at home base, Walt and Josh hoisted Mary Ellen and Olivia into two spectacular flying mounts as Nancy and Angie did handstands in front of them.

The music stopped as they assumed the ending pose. No one breathed. And then, suddenly, the room went wild, with even a few Garrison High spectators unable to keep themselves from jumping to their feet and cheering as if for their own team. A perfect end to a perfect basketball halftime. Tarenton was beating Garrison, 31 to 22.

"Pretty good if I do say so myself," Josh whispered to Nancy, as they made room for the Pompon Squad and scuttled back to the side-lines.

"If only Donny didn't look like he was going to smash the ball into someone's face," Nancy said.

Mary Ellen looked slightly chagrined, but not a whole lot. If Donny wanted to sulk and pout, that was his business. As for her, she felt she was well rid of that relationship. She'd dated him for his looks, his status, his self-assurance — and now, a week after their breakup, it was clear to her how shallow Donny really was. And how shallow she must be to have wanted someone like that so badly.

She watched him, trying not to let the others see she was watching him. As the second half wound down, he seemed to be working even harder, the sweat spraying off him every time he hurled himself into the air for a shot. Yes, he was very good at what he did. But so what? Patrick was kind and sexy and nuts about her. She had decided that this time, she'd be able to keep her relationship with him on an even keel. It wouldn't get too hot and heavy; it would just be nice and very romantic. Certainly, she hadn't changed her mind about what Patrick Henley had to offer her, but that didn't mean she had to eliminate the possibility that he might change, in time. That he might actually learn to want the same things from life that she did.

When the final basket hit home, she raced the other cheerleaders up to the front for the closing cheer. She was sparkling, exhilarated, and Tarenton's win of 59 to 42 had very little to do with it.

"Let's get the ball, now,
Move it down the court!
Never let 'em run away,
With Tarenton's sport!
Pass it, shoot it, dunk it, loot it!
Win it is our aim!
C'mon team! This is our game!
Yay!"

Mary Ellen's blonde hair flew around her head as she led the cheer. Angie looked over at her, sensing something different about her, something that hadn't been there just an hour ago. She admired Mary Ellen for so many reasons, and one of them was her ability to turn on that crowd-pleasing dazzle any time she set her mind to it. She had seen Patrick in the stands, blowing kisses and making the most ridiculous lovesick faces at Mary Ellen throughout the game. It didn't really hurt Angie that much to see it, because he did look pretty silly. But then, she remembered from her own experience with Marc months ago, love sure does make you silly — among other things.

"Boy, could I use a swim about now," Olivia sighed as they filed out the back door of the gym, avoiding the worst of the cheering crowd's crush.

"You're on," Walt agreed, putting an arm around her. "Of course," he added, feeling her soaked cotton turtleneck, "you're wet already."

"Yeah, and *you're* all wet all the time," Nancy

146

smirked. "C'mon, girls, let's race these guys to the pool."

Technically, no one was supposed to be in the Tarenton pool after school hours, but Ardith had lobbied the head of the health ed department on behalf of her kids. She liked them to work out the kinks after a game, and swimming was certainly better for them than going on a soda-and-pizza binge. Since all of them had passed the junior lifesaving course, she wasn't worried about leaving them alone at the pool.

Walt and Josh were already doing laps when the four girls staggered out into the chlorine-filled atmosphere. The Olympic-sized pool had six lanes, five for serious swimmers and one larger one for the kids who just wanted to fool around. There was a net for water volleyball strung across it, and Angie executed a neat leap over it, nearly landing on top of Josh, who was doing a slow breaststroke in the second lane. "Yow! Watch it!" he yelped.

"Sorry, Josh." Angie splashed him lightly, then ducked under the rope, back into the first lane.

"You don't have to apologize to him," Nancy laughed. She was doing her leg lifts at the shallow end, pressing against the force of the water. "He's impervious to injury." And with that, she dove underwater, swimming toward him like a shark, aiming for his legs.

"Hey, what is this? How come everybody's ganging up on me?" Josh complained, fighting off his attacker with a low feint at her waist. "Sure glad it's almost track season and I won't have to hang around with you nuts anymore."

Nancy emerged from underwater, her hair dripping, to see the four faces on the other side of the ropes frozen with apprehension. "What's that? What'd you say?" she asked. "What'd he say?" she asked Mary Ellen, who had just swum to Walt's side at the deep end and was standing with only her head sticking out of the water.

"Josh, what did you mean by that?" Olivia demanded.

He laughed nervously, then looked at all the panicked faces. "Hey, I'm not leaving tomorrow, guys. I wouldn't strand you without a sixth cheerleader. I just meant, the season's changing, and once basketball and football are over. . . ."

The group continued to stare at him, and he grew increasingly more uncomfortable with the attention. "But you don't cheer in the springtime — do you?"

"There are lots of group meets, and the statewide championships, not to mention working up new routines for next season," Mary Ellen explained as calmly as she could. "We have plenty to do in the spring."

"Josh, you couldn't. You wouldn't." Nancy shook her head. She had grown to like him so much in the past few weeks, and now, all the things she used to hate about him were rising to the surface: selfishness, arrogance.

"Look, guys, hey, you're putting me in an awful spot," Josh said, feeling really stupid just standing around in the water. He hoisted himself up on one side and sat, his legs dangling in the water. "You knew I was on the track team last

148

year, and Ardith told you I was just temporary. I mean, I've loved every minute of the cheering — well, after you all stopped being convinced that I was a klutz, I mean — and it's been terrific being part of your team. But what can I say? It's not my goal in life or anything like that."

"That means we'll have to find another guy," Angie said quietly.

"I don't think Ardith wants to do that again," Olivia cut in. "I overheard a couple of the kids on the Pompon Squad saying that if we lost another Varsity member, they might just scrap the old team and start fresh with six new people."

"They couldn't do that!" Mary Ellen was horrified by the news.

"They might," Nancy said solemnly. She looked at Josh again. "Please say you won't cut out now."

Josh wiped a few drops off his face, then looked around at their anxious faces. "I can't promise that, Nance. Sorry."

When nobody said anything, he shrugged, then grabbed his towel and walked down the side of the pool toward the exit door. He didn't look back.

"I never even dreamed he might quit," Olivia moaned.

"Me, either." Angie climbed up the steps on the shallow side and made a turban of her towel around her wet blonde hair. "Well, back to the drawing board, huh, guys? I'm going to take a long, hot shower and ponder this one." She walked to the girls' exit and disappeared quickly from the humid room.

Nancy felt awful, almost as if she were to blame for this. After all, she should have known — she could have warned them. But why hadn't Josh mentioned it to her? Because he just assumed that she knew? Shaking her head, she got out of the pool, too, and then Olivia followed suit. Nobody felt like splashing around in the water anymore.

"See you outside, Walt," Olivia said quietly as she walked past Nancy. "Give me a while to get my hair dry."

That left Mary Ellen and Walt, standing in the deep end with only their heads above water. And this was a precise mirror image of the way they both felt — up to their necks in trouble.

"Walt," Mary Ellen grimaced, "we're in the midst of a crisis."

"And I thought the whole thing was fixed. I mean, losing Pres was awful, and breaking in a new guy was tough, but this is *really* bad news."

"We've all been much too pie-in-the-sky about our future as a team," Mary Ellen said, leaning back against the soft water. She floated for a while without speaking, gazing at the ceiling of the pool room as though it might give her the answer she wanted. "The six of us — and I'm including Ardith," she continued at last, "we've all been beating ourselves to a pulp, working harder, doing more spectacular routines, hoping everything would get better. Instead, it's getting messier and messier. Sure, we've been doing great at our last few games, but nobody's going to remember that if we lose one more member. It'll mean splitting for good."

150

"You know what?" Walt said, running a hand over his water-slicked hair. "We need Pres back. And he *needs* to come back."

"Sure," Mary Ellen agreed, coming out of her float and swimming to the side of the pool, where she climbed up the ladder and sat on the edge. "So what else is new?"

"I personally don't think Pres is all that happy with his new arrangement, particularly since that wacko cousin of his moved in. His grades have been going steadily downhill — Kerry let that slip — and he seems pretty torn up about not seeing his parents. Maybe I'm imagining that part, but I don't think so. I tried to put myself in his shoes the other day, and I decided it would be damn hard to swallow my pride and go back home. But if I was miserable enough, I just might."

"Are you saying we should remind him how miserable he is?" Mary Ellen suggested, a hint of a smile on her lips.

"Not exactly. I don't think he needs any reminders. What I'm suggesting is an alternative." Walt swung up beside her by one lift of his powerful arms.

"What do you mean?"

"Well, suppose, just for argument's sake, he moved in with me? Right now, he's breaking school rules because there's no one really supervising him. As I understand it, that uncle of his is hardly ever home, so he's on his own. But if he were staying with parents of another Tarenton High kid, it should be perfectly acceptable. My folks' house is plenty big enough, and they're there all the time, except when they're around the community scouting out stories for their show. If Pres were under their wing, nobody could squawk about his breaking school rules. Even Vanessa couldn't make anything out of his living with the illustrious Manners family. What do you think?"

"Eureka!" Mary Ellen yelled, throwing her arms around his neck and toppling them both over into the water again with her enthusiasm. "That might do it. And it would only be a step away from a reconciliation with his own folks, I bet. Oh Walt, do you think your mom would agree?"

"Hey, sure. She and Dad love an audience, you know. They'll probably insist Pres go on their show some morning and talk about teenage rebellion and crime in the streets."

"You're great, Walt," Mary Ellen tossed over her shoulder, climbing up the ladder again and sprinting toward the locker room. "I can't wait to tell the others. And be sure you tell Josh everything's okay if he wants to go out for track. We're getting *Pres* back!"

Walt swam around in a slow circle, mulling over his plan. It would probably work, and Pres would probably be pretty grateful. It was even likely that Mrs. Oetjen would let him back on the squad. Only one thing bothered him, and that was such close proximity to Preston Tilford III. Walt liked being Mr. Hospitality, but he wondered if he could put a time limit on his invitation. Too much Pres around the house, as well as at school, might give him a slight inferiority complex.

He got out of the pool and dried himself off, then went to find Josh. But the locker room was empty, so he showered and dressed quickly, then grabbed his things and started for the parking lot. Olivia was waiting for him at the front door of the school building.

"You're pretty smart, you know," she said, wrapping her arms around his neck. "Mary Ellen just let the rest of us in on your brainstorm."

"Good idea, huh?"

"I think it's the best idea anyone's had yet."

He looked at her seriously, wondering about her reservations. "But. . . ?" he prodded.

She tucked her arm in his and together they walked out to the parking lot. "*But*," she admitted, "there may be a few loopholes, like Pres agreeing and your folks agreeing and Ardith and Mrs. Oetjen agreeing."

"You think it could work anyway?" he asked.

She didn't say anything. They walked to the Jeep in silence.

Angie took a deep breath and walked into the office. She waited quietly, smoothing her hair and rubbing her tongue around her teeth, just in case she'd gotten lipstick on them. She hadn't, of course, but it never hurt to check.

A young woman with dyed red hair done up in a fashionable sweep stood there staring at her. "May I help you?" she asked.

"I'd like to see Mr. Tilford, please," Angie

said in a solid voice. She didn't want to appear nervous or flustered in any way.

The secretary looked at her dubiously. "Do you have an appointment?"

"I'm afraid not," Angie stated bluntly. "But I know he'll see me. Just tell him it's about his son."

The woman paused a second, then opened the door so that Angie could step into another reception area, a wood-paneled room with huge oil paintings of clipper ships on every wall. She stood there, wishing she had something to do with her hands.

"Wait here, please. I'll see if he's free. Who shall I say wants to see him?"

"Angie . . . Angela Poletti. Uh, he doesn't know me, but I go to school with his son," she told the woman, sinking down into one of the nearest low plush leather chairs.

The secretary nodded, then left the room. Angie was too busy rehearsing her speech to look at any of the magazines that were piled neatly on the end table beside her.

So *this* was Tarenton Fabricators! The office spoke of money and hard work and power — all those things that Pres claimed to detest. And certainly she could understand his not wanting to work for his father. As crazy as she was about her mother, she knew it would be disaster if she ever started helping out at Rose Poletti's beauty parlor, in whatever capacity. Parents and children had to know where to draw the line — and working for a parent was simply out of the question as far as she was concerned. *Living* with a parent, on the other hand, was more than a necessity. It was a fact of life.

The secretary returned. "You may go in," she said briskly, showing Angie the way down the corridor. "I wouldn't take up too much of his time if I were you, though. He's a busy man," the secretary added.

Angie kept her eyes forward and walked to the door of Preston Tilford's office. A worried-looking man with steely gray hair and eyes sat before an enormous desk. There were exactly three pieces of paper cluttering it.

"Come in, please, have a seat." He rose, as he saw her stop in front of the open door.

"Thank you, Mr. Tilford. It's very kind of you to see me," Angie said in her politest tones. "It's about Pres," she went on.

"Yes, well. . . ?" He looked impatient even as he ushered her to a high-backed leather armchair and began to pace in front of the large picture window on the opposite wall.

"Mr. Tilford, Pres doesn't know I'm here, and he'd probably kill me if he did." She laughed, trying to break the tension, but got no response. "I'm one of the kids on the cheerleading squad, see. . . ."

"Oh, that group that Preston had belonged to," Mr. Tilford said with a touch — just a touch — of disdain.

"But he still does belong, you see. Oh, we got a replacement when the principal docked Pres, but it wasn't the same. You know, it's like in business," she said, fishing for a comparison Mr. Tilford would readily understand. "When you have an item that's selling, you don't try to sell something else in its place. Right?"

"I suppose so." He stopped pacing and leaned back against the windowsill, his long legs in their neatly pressed gray pin-striped pants stretching out before him. "But there's nothing I can do about that, young lady. Pres has made his choice."

Angie sighed. Now came the hard part. "Well, he did make a choice, that's true. But we all have a right to reconsider the decisions we've made. Sometimes, it just takes one push in a different direction." She looked into his face, but got nothing back. "You see, Mr. Tilford, he's not that happy living by himself, and even though he won't admit it to any of us guys on the squad, or even to Kerry, his girl friend, it's my gut feeling that he's ready to come home. The thing is, he doesn't think anyone *wants* him to come home."

"Why . . . why that's ridiculous. His mother and I have been waiting patiently all this time, and —"

"Maybe you *shouldn't* wait patiently. Maybe you should just rush in there and tell him what you feel. Not that it's my business to tell you what to do, sir," she continued hastily, "but it really would help if you'd go over to his uncle's studio and ask him back. He needs that."

Mr. Tilford looked exceedingly confused and not very pleased. "Young lady," he said, shaking his head, "in effect, you're telling me to go and beg my son to come back to the home that *he* decided wasn't good enough for him. That doesn't make much sense to me."

156

Angie was getting very exasperated. The man really was impossible. Everything had to be perfectly logical for him to get it. But if you loved your kid, you wouldn't give a flying hoot about logic. "Naturally, it's up to you. But I wish you'd go see him. Even if it's just to say hi and see how he's doing."

She got up because she had played all her cards and didn't have anything else to say. But with Preston Tilford, even the entire deck wouldn't be enough. "Thanks for your time, sir. I can find my way out."

"Nice to meet you, young lady." Mr. Tilford came around to her side of the desk, and to her surprise, he shook her hand. "It's good to know that my son has such fine friends."

"He does!" she exclaimed, and then she turned around and walked out.

All the way home in the car, Angie kept thinking about her meeting with Mr. Tilford. She hadn't really had great hopes of convincing him, but she'd thought at least that she could make a little headway for Pres. Walt's plan about living with the Manners seemed awfully half baked to her, but maybe that was because she was the kind of girl for whom family was family, and there were no intermediate steps on the way to being close with them. Other people weren't like her — she knew that — but she was certainly glad there weren't a lot of other people like Preston Tilford II, either.

CHAPTER

12

Pres hated Tuesday nights because on Tuesdays, Kerry babysat for the lady across the street who went to some adult education class. As far as Pres was concerned, adults had had all the education they needed — and they were still grossly lacking in any basic intelligence.

So on Tuesdays, Kerry had to be home for dinner early, and that meant that Pres had virtually no time alone with her. Tonight he was sitting glumly in front of the fire, wondering what to do next.

The only good thing that had happened lately was that James had been home for five days straight, long enough for him and A.J. to really get on each other's nerves. A.J. finally agreed to go back to school because he was bored out of his mind in Tarenton. Pres never mentioned the incident with Vanessa — he didn't have to. A.J. spoiled everything for himself just by sticking his big foot in his big mouth.

It got him thinking, though, about himself and his own father. Of course, the situation was entirely different: A.J. had wanted to come home, and Pres wanted to stay away from home. But did he? For all the aggravation, for all the cold looks and closed doors and the stupid fights that never went anywhere, he kind of missed the house on Fable Point. He missed his room and his old routine, and the good meals. Maybe, just possibly, he missed his parents, too. Not that he really liked them or believed that stuff about absence making the heart grow fonder. (*What heart?* he'd have said about his father.) But still and all, he got something out of that home of his. Maybe he liked the fact that being with Felicia and Preston Tilford II made him aware of how different he was from them.

He was so engrossed in his fog, he scarcely heard the sound of a car pulling up in front of James's house. Then another. He jumped up and went to the window.

Walt and Olivia led the way, and Mary Ellen came next, followed by Angie, Nancy, and that new guy, Josh. What were they doing here? He wasn't sure he wanted the new guy on the team in his house, but he couldn't very well tell him not to come in. He opened the door for them and they filed in slowly.

"Hey, guys, how's it going?" he asked cheerily. He couldn't help but notice that everyone looked extremely serious.

"Pres, we've come for a summit conference," Olivia told him grimly.

"We want you to listen and keep your trap

159

shut — if that's possible," Walt continued. "So sit down."

"Hey, what is all this?" Pres demanded, sitting cross-legged on the floor. The others sprawled out around him.

"Well, I guess it's mainly my fault," Josh said sheepishly. "I got everyone on the alert because I let them know I was going out for track again in the spring, which meant the squad would be one man short again. So after they decided they wouldn't murder me, and after Nancy reluctantly agreed to keep going out with me — even though I was a loathesome specimen of the human race — everyone figured we better come see you."

Nancy gave Josh a disparaging look, but when he put his arm around her, she sighed and relaxed into it. She couldn't stay mad at him.

"Where do things stand on your moving back home, Pres?" Mary Ellen asked quietly.

"Things stand just where they've been for the past month — in limbo," Pres shrugged.

"Not necessarily," Angie said.

"Hey, for me, nothing's changed. I'm sitting tight."

Walt took a deep breath and started talking in his low rumble, very slowly and carefully, so Pres wouldn't miss a word. "Look, how about we try this?" Walt offered. "My folks' place could be a safe house for a delinquent like you. If they take you in, you'll have a Tarenton parent looking over your shoulder. Not your parent, but close enough. Get it?"

160

"Walt, it's cool of you to ask. But I might as well just stick it out where I am. I mean, a house is a house, right?"

"No, it's not," Nancy pointed out. "This is a legitimate way to get you back on the team. We're not thinking of you — this is a pretty selfish move on our parts. And since Josh won't cooperate," she gave her boyfriend a despairing glance, *"you're* it. You have to go along with our plan. And that's that."

Pres looked at the floor, then into the bright crimson glow of the fire. "I'll think about it. I mean, I'd kill to get back on the team, but I can't see that moving in with somebody else's parents is the solution."

"There *is* another solution," Angie reminded him.

He was about to answer her when the sound of another car purring to a halt made them all look up. Pres got to his feet. He was such a motor-head, he *knew* the sound of that engine. It was his father's Mercedes, without a doubt.

"Oh boy, I can't believe this!" he muttered.

"Hey gang, time to split." Angie was with him at the window, nearly jumping up and down in her gleeful anticipation of the moment that was about to be. "See you at practice tomorrow, kid," she sang out, punching Pres playfully on the shoulder.

The others looked very confused as she led them out onto the path, steering clear of the rather determined man who was stalking up the path as if he was being pushed by a stiff wind. Angie offered a "Good-night, Mr. Tilford," as she

161

got into Josh's car after Nancy and Mary Ellen, but he didn't hear her. His mind was elsewhere.

Pres swallowed hard, then rubbed his hands on his chinos. Despite the chill air coming through the open door of the studio, he was sweating. "Hi, Dad," he said softly, looking at his father's lined face. God, he hadn't seen him in so long!

"Pres, how are you?" Mr. Tilford walked into the tiny studio, and it seemed to shrink in size as he took its measure. Funny, Pres thought, there could be seven kids in here at once and it didn't seem at all crowded. Now, however, there was scarcely room to move around.

His father stood in front of the fire for a minute, then sat on the couch, looking extremely uncomfortable. "I haven't been inside this place since just after James finished building it — what was it, ten years ago? It's not too bad, actually." He chuckled a little, but Pres could tell he was just making chit-chat for the sake of filling air space.

"How *is* James?" he asked, when his son just stood there.

"Oh, he's great. In and out a lot, you know, because he's doing so many shows these days. This is some of his stuff."

His father stared at the easel holding the painting of the green man and the blue and yellow woman in a clinch. He frowned for a second, then rolled his eyes to the ceiling. "I don't really understand modern art."

"Me, neither," Pres confessed. Well, at least they had *one* thing in common. They both thought that painting was weird.

"Pres, listen," his father began, sitting forward in his seat. "Your mother and I. . . ." He stopped, considering his words carefully. It seemed to be hard for him to get the right ones in combination, which kind of astounded Pres. He always thought of his father as right on the mark about everything.

"What I'm trying to say is," Mr. Tilford started again, "we'd like you to think about coming home. Will you?"

Pres bit his upper lip, turning away from his father. "Why should I?"

"Well, because it is your home, for one thing." Mr. Tilford heard himself beginning to sound angry, and stopped again. "And because, well, your mother misses you. And so do I," he added in a small voice.

Pres heard the words and tried to hear the meaning behind them. He couldn't let his father get away so easy. Anyhow, there had to be a catch to this. "We always fight — it's no good. And you're always jumping down my throat about every little thing I want to do. So maybe we're better off like this."

"Do you really think so? Because I don't." Mr. Tilford got up and walked over to his son, challenging him to look into those steely eyes. "I can be unreasonable, I'm aware of that. But you can be, too, you know. Like father, like son."

Pres looked at him curiously. Was that possible? Was he really just as pig-headed and stubborn as his father? "Look," he said, wanting to give a little, "I could come back for maybe a trial period, okay? But if it doesn't work out, that's it."

"I don't want any ultimatums from you," his father stated firmly. "If you're home, you're home. And we'll work things out next time."

"Like what? Like that job you were going to force me into?"

Mr. Tilford shook his head. "All right, that was a mistake. I'll admit it."

"And like my cheerleading? You think that's just about the pits, don't you?"

His father's mouth twisted as he searched for the right answer to Pres's question. "It's not what I'd choose for you, no. In my day, of course, it would have been unheard of for a young man with your potential to lead cheers at school games. But I can't deny that things have changed. And that team does seem to be made up of some nice boys and girls. Maybe cheerleading isn't the worst thing in the world, after all."

Pres's face lit up. "You mean that? I can go back on the squad?"

"If you like." His father's harsh face looked softer in the firelight, and as he started for the door, Pres had an urge to go after him. "I'll be waiting at home for you. I hope to see you within the next few hours."

But then, he felt Pres's hand on his arm and he stopped, turning to face him.

"Dad," Pres said, "I've been thinking about this for a long time. I don't really need to chew it over any more. I guess I was just waiting for you to tell me you still wanted me. Let's go home together, okay?"

The smile on his father's face was real and heartfelt. "It would be my pleasure."

"Right after we go say thanks to Uncle James for putting up with me for so long," Pres said, his own grin threatening to crack his cheeks. He knew this would be the ultimate test. His father hadn't talked to James in years, and probably had no intention of doing so now.

"Well, I. . . ." Mr. Tilford procrastinated.

"What about burying a few hatchets all at once?" Pres suggested softly.

His father hesitated for only a minute. Then he shrugged and said, "That might not be such a bad idea." Mr. Tilford laughed, knowing that his son had him where he wanted him. In his own way, Pres was just as clever a manipulator as he himself, and he was hooked. "Shall we?"

And together, matching stride for stride, they walked out of the little studio and up the path to James's house.

The away game at Wickfield was going to be tough. The Tarenton Wolves had won three straight football games, just squeaking by in the last game with a spectacular touchdown in the final seconds of play. As the crowd started filing through the gates early on that crisp Saturday afternoon, there was a feeling of expectation in the air. Would they or wouldn't they?

The Varsity team always came early so they could warm up, but today, by special arrangement with Ardith, they had done their preliminary practice in their own gym. The surprise they had in store was simply too good to spoil. So they arrived with everyone else, with little time to spare in the dressing rooms where they'd put on their uniforms and get ready to burst on the scene.

Nancy and Josh got there first, but Walt and Olivia pulled in right beside them moments after they'd picked a prime space in the Wickfield parking lot. Unfortunately, none of them saw that Vanessa had parked four cars over and was lying in wait.

"Oh, this is going to be super!" Olivia squealed, relishing the feeling of Walt's strong arms around her delicate waist.

"And what a day for it," Nancy said decisively. It was, too, with pillowlike clouds floating in a gigantic sea of azure, tinged with just a hint of rosy pink. The girls' faces were ruddy from the cold, but luckily, there was no wind at all.

"Hi, guys, are we late?" Mary Ellen and Angie piled out of Patrick's truck, and he walked them over to the group, an arm around each of them. Neither girl seemed to mind at all. Sharing was perfectly copacetic on a beautiful day like today.

"Right on time," Walt smiled, tugging Olivia forward. "But we better get moving and get changed. I can feel it in the air — we're gonna slaughter 'em today!"

"That's all very optimistic, isn't it?" they heard a husky voice say right behind them. "But as I understand it, you six will be rather down in the dumps before long. Not that I can predict the future or anything." Vanessa, dressed in her old raccoon coat with a fur cap set jauntily on her dark hair, positively gleamed with evil intent.

"Oh, do please look into your crystal ball and

166

tell us what's up, Vannie," Angie insisted, snuggling a little closer to Patrick.

"It's gotta be a beaut," Patrick chortled, "or you wouldn't look so darn smug about it."

"Well, word is out that they're going to put together a whole new cheerleading squad for the spring and summer meets and competitions. Since Pres is out and since rumor has it that Josh isn't sticking around, everybody just thought it might be better to start from scratch — maybe get all girls this time," she added pointedly.

"Oh, and who's this everybody, Vanessa?" Pres and Kerry walked up to the group, their hands linked. "Your father maybe?"

"Maybe, Pres." She gave her little catlike smile, her claws all ready to scratch.

"Oh, is that so!" Nancy sputtered. "Well, you know, Vanessa, sometimes it's better to watch and wait. Sometimes things work out."

"They certainly might for me." Vanessa tossed this statement off as lightly as she could. "I was next in line for a place on the squad, so I could very well be a shoo-in if they assembled a new one. All of you guys have had your chance anyway. You're old hat by now. The crowds are getting sick of you."

"Not as sick as we are of you, Van," Walt said disgustedly. Then he jerked his head toward the side gate of the stadium. "Let's get in there and get dressed, gang." They all marched away from the annoying presence and toward the back of the bleachers, united in their dislike of Vanessa. Then, at the doors to the dressing rooms, they split apart.

167

"Let's give that dumb kid a run for her money," Josh suggested.

"Right on," Patrick agreed.

"Be wonderful, all of you," Kerry told them with a special look in her eyes for Pres, who took his place with his team proudly.

"So tell me," Josh asked him, "what's it like living at home again?"

"Yeah," Angie chimed in. "Can you bear it?"

He looked around at the circle of friends who were his closest allies. "You know," he said slowly, "it's not as bad as I remembered. Maybe being with my folks isn't such a terrible idea — for another year, anyhow."

They all turned at the sound of Ardith, slightly out of her mind, who nearly screeched as she approached them. "Aren't you ready yet? The game's about to start, for heaven's sake!" They scattered fast, making tracks toward their respective dressing rooms.

The stands were filled and waiting when the Tarenton Varsity team raced onto the field. And then, an audible cheer went up as the crowd saw the team's lineup. It was Mary Ellen at the forefront, followed by Walt, Olivia, Angie, and Nancy. Pres Tilford brought up the rear! With a death-defying set of cartwheels and aerial spins, he sat every person in the bleachers on their ear. The girls did banana jumps around him, making way for his next tumbling feat, which was a triple back flip followed by a stag leap. He came out of the move to a standing ovation, and he knew he deserved it. All the energy that had been bottled in him for so long was spilling out now, all over the whole stadium. Even when the football players ran out, their names booming over the loudspeaker system, the crowd's eyes were still on him.

The music started and the cheerleaders took their places.

> "What's the ticket to VICTORY?
> It's power, skill, and ENERGY!
> We're the best — now don't say no,
> Give us a hand and let us GO!

> "Down that field! Move it on down!
> Start the game, let's go to town!
> Tarenton's a winner, can't be beat!
> Knock their socks right off their feet!

>> "Give it all you got!
>> Tarenton's hot!
>> Yeah, team! W-I-N!"

Patrick, Josh, and Kerry looked down from the stands, yelling themselves hoarse. They watched the scarlet and white uniforms flash, the high kicks and spins making both colors run together against the brilliant blue sky. Mary Ellen, Angie, Nancy, Walt, Olivia, and Pres had something indefinable, something so special it couldn't be tampered with. They were a team . . . for better or for worse. They knew what the better was, but they wondered if they'd seen the worse.

Can one wild party change Olivia's life? Read Cheerleaders #7, FLIRTING.

Join the Team!

They're talented. They're fabulous-looking. They're winners! And they've got what you want! Don't miss any of these exciting CHEERLEADERS books!

Watch for these titles! $2.25 each

Books chosen with you in mind from

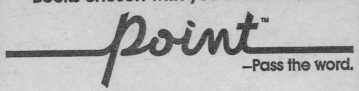

—Pass the word.

Living...loving...growing.
That's what **POINT** books are all about!
They're books you'll love reading and
will want to tell your friends about.

Don't miss these other exciting **Point** titles!

NEW POINT TITLES! $2.25 each